Savor Me

Master Chefs #2

Kailin Gow

Savor Me (The Master Chefs Series #2)

Savor Me (The Master Chefs Series #2)
Published by Sparklesoup Inc.
Copyright © 2013 Kailin Gow

For information, please contact:

Sparklesoup Inc.
www.sparklesoup.com
First Edition.
Printed in the United States of America.

DEDICATION

This dedication is for all women who believe in second chances.

Prologue

"Over here, Miss Taryn Cummings."

Caught in the busy come and go of JFK airport, Taryn turned to see her brother in the crowd, waving her over. He flashed her a mocking grin. Forcing a smile, she waved and maneuvered her way to him. "Bobby," she said as she gave him a hug. "What are you doing here? Mom made you come out and get me, huh?"

He kissed her cheek and took her suitcase. "Hey, what an opinion you have of your little brother. I offered to come."

"Yeah, I know how you love to drive through traffic, wrestle into a parking space and elbow your way through this crowd... all to come and help me lug my suitcase back out... How far are you parked?"

Chuckling, he put his arm around her shoulder and escorted her out. "It's a beautiful day for a walk in the Big

A. I'm sure after being cooped up in that plane for hours, a little fresh air will do you good."

Shielding his eyes from the blinding sun, he stopped and looked out at the field of cars. "Now, if only I could remember where I left that big, black sucker."

Taryn looked at him. "Mom let you take her Lexus?"

"Hey, I'm offended. You say that like I'm not trustworthy." He continued to scan the parking lot.

"Seriously, Bobby. Where d'you park it?"

He nudged her playfully with his elbow and turned to the left. Sooner than he'd let on, they arrived at the large SUV. After tossing her suitcase into the back seat, they got in and drove off.

"So?"

"So?"

"How's my driving?"

"Your driving? I just came home from months in France and you want me to comment on your driving?"

"Ever since you got in the car, you've been checking my blind spot, looking behind us, making sure I make a full stop. Relax, *ma grande soeur*, I know how to drive."

"And you've been learning a bit of French, too?"

"Well, you've been there so long, I thought maybe you wouldn't understand English anymore." He laughed at himself.

"You're such a silly goof."

"Ha, that's not what Kristy said last night."

Taryn leaned her head back into the headrest. "Please, spare me the details of your torrid love life."

"It's not torrid. It's just busy."

She turned to look at him. "I must admit, *mon petit frere*, you do look good." She reached out to finger a blond lock that lightly brushed against the nape of his neck. "You let your hair grow in a bit."

"Yeah... the girls love it."

Taryn laughed. "I imagine they would. So, besides staying busy with the ladies, what you been up to?"

"Still taking those cooking classes at college. You know, girls love that, too. Do you know how much girls are turned on by a guy who knows how to cook?"

"Yeah," Taryn droned. "Tell me about it."

"And at my age. I mean, girls don't expect a good looking, eighteen year old guy to be so talented in the kitchen... you know what I mean?"

"You're an eternal flirt, you know that?"

"Yep."

"And so humble."

"I do what I can. Besides, false humility never did anybody good."

Taryn snorted. "What about the restaurant?"

"Busy. I'm there more than thirty hours a week now."

"Thirty? And when do you go to college?"

"Pretty much the rest of the time. I have to admit, between running the kitchen and keeping my grades up, I don't have much time to fool around."

Taryn grinned and affectionately patted his hand. "I'm sure you manage to find time."

Glancing at her, he flashed her his killer smile.

No wonder the girls all fall for him, she thought. *He is pretty darn cute.*

"You know, now that you've dropped all this Paris business, why don't you take a course with me at college."

"I don't think so. I'm going to concentrate on giving mom a hand at the restaurant. The hours I put in will give you a break."

"Ah, come on. It'd be fun. I mean, I know it's not a Parisian institute or nothing, but it's a decent course. I've already learned a lot. And not just about cooking. I'm taking a restaurant management course now."

"Thanks, Bobby, but I honestly can't imagine working with you most of the day then going off to take the same classes as you. I think a sibling relationship can only take so much togetherness."

Looking straight ahead, he snorted. "Yeah, I think you're right."

As they drove in front of La Benicoise, one of the restaurants Errol had opened in New York, Taryn's heart skipped a beat. She'd managed to put him out of her mind the entire twenty minutes she'd spent catching up with Bobby, but now the thought of him struck her unexpectedly and knocked the air out of her.

"You okay?"

"Huh?"

"You gasped out of nowhere. What's up?"

"Nothing. Just surprised by how things have changed since I've been gone."

"Really? Cause you just went pale like a ghost. Besides, you haven't been away that long and the neighborhood hasn't changed that much. I mean they finished repairing the water main on twenty-fifth, but that's about it."

She hated lying to him, but there was no way she could share her thoughts with him. How could she tell him about the wild nights she spent with Errol, the crazy things he made her do, the wild things that brought her so much pleasure?"

"So how was that Chef Errol King?"

Damn it. Taryn shuddered. Sometimes she'd swear her little brother could read right through her.

He was fine, she wanted to say. Great. Arousing. Erotic. Exciting. He was more handsome than a man had the right to be. He was more thrilling than anything she'd ever known.

And damn it, she'd let herself fall so hopelessly in love with a man who only saw her as another sex toy, another play thing.

"He's a better chef than he is a teacher," she finally said.

"Really. Did you learn a lot from him anyway?"

I'll say. "Yeah, sure. I mean the guy's got experience. He knows his way around the kitchen."

- 9 -

"Is he as hard on his students as I've heard he is?"

"He doesn't have much patience for silliness. If you're not paying attention and getting it right, you have no business being in his class."

"Then it's probably not the right class for me," Bobby said with a playful grin.

"You wouldn't last five minutes in one of his classes." Taryn laughed, though her heart wasn't in it.

"Is he the reason you came back? I mean, was he too hard on you?"

Yes and yes. "No. I think it was a combination of being homesick, struggling with the language and dealing with a new substitute teacher we got mid course. She was a real doozy. All lunatic and barely anything pertinent to teach us." She turned to look out the window. "Pastry puff, my ass," she muttered as she remembered the sexy goddess who'd ruined pastry for her forever.

Chapter 1

Taryn lay back on her bed and closed her eyes. It was just half a lie, she told herself.

Jet lag. Hardly slept on the plane. The change in temperature. The change in scenery. The change in language. After discussing her return home with her mom for a brief ten minutes, Taryn had quickly disengaged herself from the conversation and sought the shelter and solace of her old room. While she wasn't nearly as tired as she claimed, she desperately needed a moment alone to collect her thoughts.

She pulled out her phone and read and re-read every one of Errol's texts. She'd yet to answer any of them. Again, she re-read the last one.

Fine. If that's the way you want it, I'm coming after you. I'm on the next flight to New York. I'll find you, Taryn. I'll find you and bring you back to Paris.

She'd had plenty of time to consider her response, but it'd constantly changed. Yes. No. Maybe. Not now. Not ever. Why?

Finally she decided on an answer. *Errol, please don't come to New York. I need to be alone and I don't want to spend my time looking over my shoulder afraid I'll run into you.*

She pressed *send* and put her phone down. Maybe she'd waited too long. Maybe he was already on his way to New York.

Her phone signaled a new text. With lightning speed, she picked up her phone and looked at the text.

I'm at the airport. My flight leaves in twelve minutes. Do you really want me to turn around and forget about going to New York? Forget about you?

Her heart skipped a beat. Her body craved his touch and she knew she was hungry to have him, to taste him.

I think it's best for now.

She waited for his response, breathless and anxious. A part of her wanted him to come regardless of her request.

If that's really what you want, okay. I'll respect your wishes. But, Taryn, your studies, you have such talent, so much potential. How can you let all that slip away from you? Doesn't it mean anything to you?

She couldn't deny how important it was to her, but even if she returned to Paris now, she'd never be able to concentrate enough to get through a single class.

I'll get back to my studies when the time is right. For now I need to be here, with my family, helping at the restaurant.

Truth was she would probably wait until he left Paris and no longer taught at the Institute before going back.

I understand. I'll leave you alone. I hope you'll let me know when you're ready to talk to me again.

She should be elated. He was showing such respect for her wishes. Yet all she felt was dismayed, and disappointed. She regretted so much…In the turmoil of her emotions, she didn't know if she'd ever be ready to talk to him again and hesitated before answering him.

Yes, of course. I'll let you know. Bye, Errol

Chapter 2

Still groggy from her first night in New York, Taryn opened her eyes a crack. Someone was noisily rattling dishes in the kitchen, obviously oblivious to the fact she was trying to get some sleep. Taryn peered at her alarm clock. Four o'clock. *My God, who's up at this hour?*

Coffee percolated, toast jumped out of the toaster and something was sizzling in a frying pan. *Clink*; a cup set in a saucer. *Swish*; coffee heading into that cup. *Tink, tink, tink*; the spoon going round and round... and round and round.

Mom, Taryn thought. No one stirred coffee as persistently as Samantha Cummings.

Though she longed to stay curled up in bed with her pillow tucked neatly in her arms, Taryn got out of bed, set her feet into her fuzzy slippers and threw on her favorite old, ratty robe.

"Hey, Mom." She squinted as she entered the blinding light of the kitchen. "What you up to?"

"Same old, same old, Taryn. Breakfast?"

Taryn tried not to frown. "No, I'm still digesting dinner."

"Lost the habit of getting up in the morning, huh? I heard Parisians have dinner at nine o'clock at night. What time do they get up? Noon?"

"Mom, it's four o'clock. The birds aren't even up yet."

Samantha grinned as she examined her daughter. "It's good to have you home, Taryn. I don't know what happened out there, and maybe you'll let me in on it one day, but I'm happy you're here."

"Me, too, Mom."

"Good. Then go get dressed, grab a cup of coffee and a toast and let's go."

"Now?"

"Honey, I have a few deliveries coming in at five. Thirty pounds of beef, fifteen pounds of pork, twenty whole chickens, twenty-five loaves of bread, ten pounds of butter. Then we've got carrots, potatoes, rice, onions... oh, damn, I forgot to order the onions. Ah, well... And I also have a few specialty items coming in... a few new recipes we're trying."

"Really? I can't wait to taste them."

"Hope you'll have time. Once the deliveries arrive we'll barely have half an hour to put it all away before the breakfast crowd comes in."

"I'll take two coffees then."

"You bet."

Seven minutes later they were in the darkened restaurant waiting for the first delivery truck.

"Sorry I woke you up so early. I guess it was a rude awakening."

"That's okay, Mom. I had intended to come in to help you."

"Yeah… I know. I had told myself I wouldn't push you to come in so fast, but truth is…" She nudged Taryn playfully. "I've missed you, honey."

They had little time to say more. The deliveries arrived, they stacked everything away neatly and, as predicted, the morning crowd arrived. They'd barely cleared everything away when they learned one of the waitresses wouldn't be in for the noonday shift, leaving Taryn to help out on the floor.

Though worn out, Taryn realized as she looked at her watch at four thirty that she'd not had a chance to think of Errol. Good, she thought. All the better.

Sitting down for a brief moment to rub her feet, she looked out at the early dinner crowd. The stream of people coming and going was relentless. She hadn't stopped since they'd arrived so early that morning.

"Think you can hang on until Bobby arrives?" Samantha said. She put her hand to her daughter's shoulder.

"Sure, Mom."

"I hate to cut into your break, but I need someone to separate that order of meat we got this morning."

"That was this morning? Geez, it's seems like such a long time ago. I thought that was yesterday."

"Cute, dear. Can I count on you to do this for me?"

"Yeah. I'm on it now."

Two hours later she stepped out of the refrigerator bloody and exhausted.

"Is the rush over?" she asked her mom.

"Almost. Just a few late arrivals. Most of them just want dessert and coffee or a light dinner."

- 17 -

"Want me to go out and help Rhonda?" She pulled off her soiled jacket.

"I think she'd appreciate that. She's been out there alone for the past hour. Marla left early."

Taryn grabbed a pad and pencil and headed to the section Marla usually worked. In the corner, a lone, blond young man sat looking at the menu.

"The rib eye is particularly good tonight," she offered.

The young man set the menu on the table and looked up at her.

"Matt!"

"Taryn!"

"What are you doing here? I thought you'd moved to Philadelphia."

"And I thought you were in Europe."

"I just got in yesterday."

"And your mom already has you working the floor?"

"We're having trouble with a few waitresses. What are you doing in town?"

He pinched his blue t-shirt. "FDNY."

"A firefighter, huh. Impressive."

"Hey, you have time to sit and have coffee with me?"

Taryn looked around. A couple sat at one table near the window, while a trio of young women sat consoling a fourth who was visibly heartbroken. Near the back two lone men sat at separate tables. "I only have a few tables to wait on, then I'm all yours."

He grinned and Taryn was caught off guard by the tingling sensation that quickly filled her gut. Matt had always been a good looking guy, in a very sweet and boyish way, but now... His biceps tore at the fabric of his t-shirt, his chest was broad and strong, his chin masculine and assertive, and his piercing blue eyes... they beckoned her.

"Be right back," she said with a grin. As Taryn hurried to serve the other clients, her mind jumped forward, imagining all the things she could do with the handsome and sexy fireman.

Damn, Taryn. Fireman fantasies. That's so cliché.

I don't care, she thought with a wicked grin. *He's good looking, he's sexy as all get out, and damn if he doesn't want me. He's always had a crush on me.*

As she set a piece of cherry pie and coffee in front of the old man sitting alone, she gazed at Matt. His eyes had followed her every move since she'd left his table.

"I'm just going to bring that teary-eyed girl a few napkins then I'm all yours," she said as she passed him by.

She came back a few moments later and sat down across from him. "I haven't seen you since... well, since high school graduation. You've grown into a very handsome man. A very ruggedly handsome man."

He snorted shyly. "Thanks."

"I never knew you wanted to be a firefighter."

"Neither did I, actually. I mean I played with fire trucks when I was a kid and stuff, but I never really thought about making a career of it. 9/11 scared the shit out of me. I had nightmares about that for months after. I never would have thought I'd end up where I am now."

"So what made you do it?"

He shrugged. "You remember Clark? That tall, gangly guy who always looked like he'd just gotten out of bed?"

"The one who always looked like he'd taken a dump in his jeans?"

"Yeah, that one," he said with a chuckle.

"I bumped into him one day a few months after graduation. I mean, I still didn't really know what I wanted to do with my life and I was just hanging around, going from one meaningless and meager paying job to another. So, anyway, Clark tells me he's on his way to the Fire Academy on Randall's Island. I had nothing better to do that day and I was intrigued so I went along with him. Four years later, here I am."

"Must've been hard."

"Eighteen weeks of the hardest work I'd ever done. I never thought firefighting was so technical. I thought you just went in with a hose and that was it; drown the sucker. We had a course in Fire Science. Really interesting stuff. And of course you have to be in good physical condition to keep up with all this, and they really whip you into shape. They have a challenge course, work outs and we'd run three miles every day."

"No wonder you look so great."

"Thanks."

He flexed his biceps and Taryn wondered if it was an involuntary reaction to her compliment or an intended attempt to show off.

"I'll admit, all that hard work paid off. Besides, turns out I really like it. There's something about going in and fighting that beast that really gets to me."

"That's really cool. I'm happy for you. And I bet you also have all the girls wanting you to come in and save them."

"Yeah, you know I thought that was all myth and rumors and exaggerated stories, but it's true. A lot of women fantasize… well, you know."

"Why, Matt Mininger. Are you blushing?" She reached out to playfully tap his hand.

He quickly took advantage of the move and gripped her fingers in his. "I can honestly say, I've never benefited from that fantasy."

"You're a good looking guy, Matt. I'm sure it's not for lack of offers."

Grinning, he took her hand fully into his. "I'm happy I ran into you. It's a very pleasant surprise. Taryn."

"I'm happy to see you, too." As the words came out, she suddenly thought of Errol. He'd changed so much of who she was and how she viewed men. Looking at Matt now, she couldn't help but wonder what he looked like under that firefighter blue. She wondered if he was gentle, romantic and giving, or was he a ravenous animal who liked it rough, liked it loud, liked it a little on the painful side.

"What about you? I bet you got a ton of marriage proposals from those suave Frenchmen."

Proposal, yes, but not for marriage. "I didn't really have time to socialize much. I was taking some pretty heavy duty cooking classes in a culinary institute and it didn't leave me with much free time. Whenever I wasn't in class, I was at home in the kitchen working on some new technique or a new recipe idea I'd had. I thought I knew a lot about cooking until I learned how little I knew. In addition to that, getting around Paris wasn't always easy. I came to know a few of the streets between where I lived and the institute, but not much beyond that. And besides, the language barrier made it a little complicated. You know, just when you think you've said 'no' to a guy's invitation, it turns out you just said you were free to see him." She realized she was saying too much, and making too many excuses, but couldn't stop herself. "The weather was nice, though, for the most part and I did have the chance to take in a museum or two. And of course the Eiffel Tower. The elevator ride up is spectacular, and, did you know there's a restaurant up there? Really nice. A special place to..." Her voice cracked as she was engulfed in a sudden wave of emotion.

That day with Errol, it'd been so amazing. Was that the day she'd truly fallen for him? Was that the day she saw beyond the brash chef and the harsh professor, and simply saw a beautiful man?

Yes, the beautiful man who, in the end, wanted only a fuck buddy.

"You okay?" Matt squeezed her hand.

With her free hand she wiped away a stray tear. "Oh, I guess Paris affected me more than I realized," she said with a shaky voice. "It's so easy to get caught up in the romanticism of it all. I guess I miss it more than I expected."

"You know, New York has some pretty fascinating places, too."

She chuckled. "Yeah, I know. Don't get me wrong. I'm happy to be back."

"I bet I could show you a few places in New York that you never even knew about... some pretty fantastic and, yes, even romantic places."

"You're sweet, Matt." She quickly caught the dismay in his eyes. What guy wants to be called sweet by the girl he has a crush on? "I appreciate you trying to cheer me up."

"If you give me a chance, I think I could make you forget all about Paris."

She looked directly into his eyes and was surprised by the intensity behind them. Maybe he wasn't so sweet after all. "You know what? I might just take you up on that offer."

Chapter 3

Though that first day at the restaurant nearly had Taryn crawling home on all fours, she managed to pace herself better the next day. She went to bed earlier than she had gotten into the habit of in Paris, and cut out the wine with dinner.

Within that first week, she'd fallen into a routine that was exhilarating and fulfilling. On weekends, she shared duties with Bobby, while during the week she swapped places. They were like a pro-wrestling tag team, one coming in just as the other had to leave.

They both knew the other's strengths and weaknesses and therefore prepared the kitchen accordingly. Taryn prepared the sauces, which always gave Bobby a hard time, while Bobby took care of some of the heavier work, like tending to the larger pots and pans, and dealing with cuts of beef.

Matt came in regularly and always had a cute and flirtatious word to say to her.

"So when are you going to take me up on my offer?" he'd said after three weeks. He'd sneaked a peek into the kitchen and caught her as she sautéed mushrooms with one hand and grilled a steak with the other. Leaning casually against the doorjamb, he'd looked her over.

"Matt," Taryn had chastised, "you can't just walk in here and give me the once over while I have a full plate in my hands. I'm likely to make a mess... an expensive mess."

"Fair enough," he said with his usual wicked grin. "But it's nice to know I have that effect on you."

As she put the finishing touch to the plate she was preparing, Taryn smiled at the thought of him. He'd quickly become the soothing balm that eased the pain of her breakup with Errol, and she always looked forward to seeing him. She'd come to know his shifts at the fire house by heart.

He'd worked the day shift that day and would probably be stopping by for dessert and that persistent invitation to visit New York. Some day she would have to set aside a bit of time to spend with him outside the walls of the restaurant.

"Taryn," Samantha called out. "Someone liked your whiskey braised cutlet so much, they want to thank you in person. Table six."

"Really?" Excited by the response to her new recipe, Taryn took her prepared plate and nodded at Marla. "I'll take this one out. Table twelve, right?"

"Right."

Taryn flowed through the crowded restaurant, proud of how things had been going since she'd come back. The place had grown busy while she'd been in Paris, and had grown busier still since her return. The few new items she'd added to the menu had been highly praised and well received.

With the proud disposition of the finest chef in the fanciest restaurant, she arrived at table twelve, served the waiting patron with a smile and a quick 'bon appetite' and headed to table six for her much needed pat on the back. Giddy like a child awaiting his trophy at the end of a relay race, she tried to contain her explosive smile.

"Hello, sir. You wanted to see me about..." Her jaw dropped and her heart flipped over three times in quick succession. "Errol." She didn't know if she was pleased or angry.

His eyes widened in obvious surprise. "Taryn?!" He instantly stood and extended his arms to take her then awkwardly retracted them and left them hanging at his side. "You? Here? I... And you did..." He gestured toward his empty plate. "You're the one who...?"

A few other patrons had turned to look their way. "Yes," she said demurely. "I learned a lot of what I know and put to use here while I was in Paris."

He grinned, his playful gaze taking her in, drinking her up and savoring the sight of her. "You..." As his disbelieving gaze continued to sweep over her, he swallowed and seemed at a loss for words. "You look wonderful. Radiant, actually."

The softness of his voice, filled with regret, touched her, but she remained wary. "What brings you to New York?"

"I have to make an appearance at La Benicoise tomorrow night." He shrugged with annoyance. "Part of the perks and peeves of owning a world renowned restaurant."

She glanced around her own busy restaurant. "Yeah... perks and peeves."

"I wonder if... You're working. You must be pretty busy. I... Maybe later..."

"Thank you for respecting my decision, Errol," she said as she sensed where he was going.

He cleared his throat and seemed uncharacteristically uncomfortable. "Of course. And... I hope you don't think I planned..."

"No. I know La Benicoise isn't too far from here. I guess I should feel honored you stopped here when you have so many places to choose from."

"A happy accident all due to a bellhop."

"A bellhop?"

"I asked him where the hottest new restaurant was and he said Sam's."

"Really? Wow. How cool is that?"

"Pretty cool, I'd say." He smiled, warm and engaging.

Her heart ached and she longed to reach out and touch him, but feared all the emotions that would come with it. "Look," she said as she shot a quick glance around the restaurant. "I have to get back to work. We're in near chaos back there. Enjoy your stay in New York."

She turned to leave, but he lightly set his hand on her forearm to stop her. The jolt of electricity that shot through her almost knocked her off her feet. How could a man possibly have such an effect on a woman? It was pure insanity.

"I was hoping to have dessert. What do you recommend?"

Taryn glanced at his hand then swept her gaze up his arm, over his shoulder and finally met his heated gaze. "We have a lot of fancy, shmancy stuff, but despite all that, my favorite is our mile high apple pie."

"Sounds good."

Taryn hesitated then nodded. "I'll bring you a slice in a minute." As she walked away she noticed Matt had come in and was being seated at table ten. He immediately waved her over.

"Hey, how you doing tonight?" He had a broad and genuine smile, though he looked tired and weary.

"Hectic, but the dinner rush is almost over. I heard sirens blaring earlier. Sounds like you guys were pretty busy, too."

"Yeah, it's been one of those days. I'm looking forward to a nice, relaxing evening." He paused a moment.

"Look, I don't know if you're into constellations and stars and all that, but we're set to have a clear night and they say we should have a nice view of a comet that's passing by. We could drive out to Long Island and…"

"That sounds so cool, Matt," she cut in, "but I don't know when I'll get off. Bobby's been bogged down with exams and I probably won't get out of here before closing."

He reached out to take her hand, his fingers gently playing along hers. "You're going to burn yourself out working so hard."

"I'm young. I can handle it," she said with a wry smile. "Can I bring you anything?"

"I can't seem to get enough of that mile high."

"Coming right up."

Taryn hurried to the kitchen, sliced two hefty wedges of pie and set them each on a dessert plate.

"Want me to take care of that?" Marla offered.

"Naw, I got it." Taryn returned to the dining room. "Here you go, Matt." She set the pie down in front of him and barely gave him a chance to say thank you before going on to Errol's table.

The moment she saw him she knew he wasn't pleased.

"What was that?" His tone was pleasant, but barely.

"This is the pie you asked for."

"Not this… that." He jutted his chin toward Matt.

"Matt's an old school friend."

"And Matt is in the habit of holding your hand?"

"Matt is in the habit of being a sweet and charming guy." She turned and walked away, but instantly heard Errol's footsteps behind her.

Please don't make a scene here? she silently begged. *Not in front of my mother. Not in front of all these people.*

Before reaching the kitchen, Errol nudged her through the partition that separated the main dining room from the private dinner hall. Used occasionally for private parties and large gatherings, the large, empty room was now dark and still.

"What are you doing?" Taryn whispered as Errol pushed her up against the wall. "I don't have time for this, Errol."

"Really? You don't have time for this?" He kissed her, hard and passionate, possessing her. His hands roamed over her body and stopped to cup her breasts.

"Errol," she breathed through his kisses.

"I've missed you, Taryn." His lips played over the skin of her neck and worked their way into the opening of her shirt. "Damn, Taryn. Tell me you don't miss this. Tell me you haven't thought of my touch."

Just seconds away from succumbing, from admitting how badly she wanted him, she heard the back door at the far end of the dinner hall open. She stiffened and shoved Errol's hands out of her shirt.

Through the gloom she could barely make out Bobby's silhouette as he came in to work. With Errol's aroused and arousing body pressed against her, she silently watched her brother pass along the far wall that cut straight into the kitchen. Only when he was gone did she breathe again.

"You have to go," she hissed at Errol.

"Your body betrays you, Taryn. You want me... just as much as I want you."

"What my body wants and what my heart wants are two different things, Errol. Anyone could touch my body and bring a spark of arousal."

"Anyone? Like that Matt kid? Come on, Taryn. What is he, a firefighter?"

"As a matter of fact, he is."

"You're too good for that cliché, Taryn."

"Thanks for your opinion, but if you don't mind, I think I'm quite capable of discerning who's good for me and who isn't."

She turned to walk out, but Errol grabbed her arm and pulled her to him. His lips covered hers and brought a warm sensation that quickly traveled through her body and grew with heated intensity. His tongue filled her mouth and her body screamed out its need to be fully satisfied. There was something different in his kiss... something softer, gentler.

He groaned with desire, with a hunger that had never been there before, with an emotion that...

No, she wouldn't allow her thoughts to go there. There were no emotions. He was incapable of true emotion. This was just pure sexual desire; just pure lustful arousal.

Despite every logical thought that tried to pierce her mind, she wrapped her arms around him and crushed her breasts to his chest. His erection pressed against her belly and she knew she wanted more.

He pulled away suddenly, leaving her cold and aching as he headed to the partition. "Now tell me who's better for you." And he walked out.

Chapter 4

Sleep refused to come as thoughts of Errol repeatedly played in Taryn's head. *Why did he have to show up like that? Why did he have to walk into my restaurant?*

"Why did he have to look so damned good?" she muttered.

Her body was on high alert, eager for stimulation, desperate for satisfaction. No matter what logic she tried to bring to the hunger she felt, her need to be sated refused to diminish.

She glanced at her clock radio; two twenty-seven. How could she possibly be as exhausted as she felt and still remain awake half the night?

Frustrated, she threw the covers off and got out of bed. Neglecting to be mindful of those who slept, she stomped across the floor of her room and pulled back the curtain just enough to peek out the window.

A few late night walkers, runners and stalkers roamed the streets. At the corner, a streetlight threatened to burn out. All things considered, it was pretty quiet.

New York; her home. The Bronx; how in the world could a girl from the Bronx fall in love with a chef in Paris?

In love? Really? You're kidding yourself. She pulled the curtain back a little further, though she had no idea what she was looking for.

The thrill. The excitement. Paris.

No, she thought with a sober shake of her head. *The thrill and excitement of Errol.* He was the one who'd rid her of her naïve view of the world, her innocent disposition. He was the one who'd thrown open Pandora's box, and now she had no idea how to close it.

Closing her eyes, she leaned her forehead against the cool glass and remembered their kiss. She'd thought of little else since then. Every other minute she'd licked her lips, tasted his breath, and had wanted to scream for want of him.

Tears lined her lashes as she realized it wasn't just her body that screamed out for him. It wasn't just lust she felt for him… and she hated herself for it.

She hated how she revered him, looked up to him, respected him as a chef and man of the world. She hated how she admired his talent in the kitchen, how she envisioned his ease with literally every culinary technique.

But more than anything, she hated how she enjoyed being with him, having dinner with him, laughing with him.

She'd left New York a sweet and innocent girl and Errol had taught her what being a woman truly meant.

Yeah, she thought with bitterness. *Being a woman sucks.*

"Damn it, Errol. Why did you make me fall in love with you?" she muttered against the window pane. When she opened her eyes and saw the mist her breath had brought to the glass, she couldn't resist the adolescent impulse to draw a heart. "I love you, Errol."

With the unrequited declaration hanging in the air of her bedroom, Taryn returned to her bed and, after much turning and twisting, finally found sleep… forty minutes before her alarm went off.

"Hey, pumpkin," Samantha said as Taryn entered the kitchen. "I didn't expect to see you up so early."

"I've been getting up at five-thirty since that first day, Mom."

"Yeah, but you didn't sleep very much, did you?"

"How d'you know?"

"I heard you pounding the floor."

"Sorry. I should've tiptoed."

"Want a ride with me, or you want to take it easy and come in a little later."

"You know I can't do that. Hopefully you'll get a bit of traffic and I'll catch a few Zs on the way."

"Forever the pragmatic."

They made it to the restaurant without much delay and were soon caught up in the morning rush.

When things settled down a bit, Samantha came to see Taryn who was helping put away pots and pans. "Honey, I need you to run out to the market."

Taryn stopped to look at her and Sam ran her fingers through her daughter's hair. "You look like you could use a breath of fresh air anyway."

"Sure. What do you need?"

"Fresh herbs, mostly. Check out the lemons and limes, too. There's a guy down there – Mehmet – he has some really great spices, things we don't usually use. I go to him every once in a while and try something new. Tell him I sent you and he'll know what I haven't tried yet.

You'll find him down at the corner near the girl who's always there selling flowers."

"Anything else?" Taryn headed for the back door and reached for her jacket that hung on a hook.

"If the grapefruit looks good, get a few… four or five, and a few pineapples, but only if they're ripe."

"Got it. I'll be back in a bit."

The minute she stepped outside, she realized just how right her mother was. The cool fresh air and dazzling sunshine felt great on her skin. Though still sluggish from lack of sleep, her spirits rose as she arrived at the hustle and bustle of the Farmers' Market.

At the first stand she found the lemons and limes to her liking and bought six of each. As she meandered through the next few stands, she picked up a few grapefruits and two pineapples.

The scent of fresh herbs brought her to her next stop. She set her heavy bag of grapefruits and pineapples on the ground, picked up a parcel of parsley and sniffed it.

"Freshly cut this morning," the vendor said.

Smiling, Taryn looked at him. "Sure smells like it." But her smile quickly faded as she spotted a familiar figure just behind him.

At a stand selling exotic and rare mushrooms, Errol stood with a breathtaking redhead at his side.

Long and luscious locks played along Errol's shoulder as the vixen leaned into him. Her hand ran along the waist of his jeans then slipped down to pat his behind.

Though Errol pulled away slightly, he turned to her with a brilliant smile that declared just how much he enjoyed her touch.

Taryn wanted to vomit. Not here. How dare he come and flaunt a new conquest right here in her backyard. Feeling flushed and queasy, she wanted to run, wanted to hide. She wanted anything but to face him with… that.

Too late. He turned and looked directly at her as if he'd sensed her presence. A smile slowly warmed his face as he drank her in.

Taryn paid for her parsley and tried to think of an excuse for a quick retreat. Errol headed her way, the auburn-haired siren at his heels.

"Errol," Taryn said when she realized she couldn't escape the inevitable. "What are the chances of running into you here?"

"I was just thinking the same thing." He grinned, that boyish grin that made her want to run her fingers through his hair, press her body to him and passionately kiss his lips.

Waving her parcel of parsley, she said, "My mom needed a few things." She tossed the parcel into her bag of lemons and lime, and picked up the bag of grapefruits and pineapples.

"It's a nice market. I remember coming here a lot when I first opened the restaurant."

Taryn tried to concentrate on his words, but was infuriatingly distracted by the obvious adoration of the buxom beauty at his side. What was he doing with a woman like that? She was unabashedly leaning into him, practically pawing him. Didn't he want a woman who offered more of a challenge?

Annoyed by the whole scene, Taryn clucked her tongue, and after a quick sidelong glance at the brazen woman looked up at Errol. "Yeah, right. Whatever."

"Oh," Errol said with a nervous fidget. "Taryn, I don't think you know Suzanne Phipps. She's the Executive Chef at La Benicoise."

Great. They work together, Taryn thought as she withheld the urge to gag. "Oh, how nice. Well..." She looked around, seeking a way out of the awkward encounter.

"Suzanne, this is Taryn Cummings. She was a student of mine in Paris."

A student? Was that all their relationship had been? She'd now been rendered the meager status of having been his student?

Suzanne extended a fluttering hand with meticulously manicured fingernails to Taryn. "I've always wondered what kind of teacher Errol was." Her voice was pure sultry.

Taryn swallowed the bile that'd collected at the back of her throat as she looked up into perfectly porcelain face. Deep green eyes looked back at her, almost daring her.

"Never mind my talents as a teacher," Errol shot in. "What's important is the success rate of my restaurants."

Suzanne smiled, her pulpy red lips visibly aching to connect with Errol's. Taryn didn't even want to think of her own stringy strands of hair that'd been hastily pulled back into a haphazard ponytail. The comfort-fit jeans she wore to work were unflattering, and her shirt was slightly soiled.

Yes, she thought with disgust. She was the perfect Quasimodo to Errol's Esmeralda. She was the pumpkin next to his princess. She was the old, busted up Edsel to his shiny new Corvette.

With a victorious glint in her eye, Suzanne turned to inspect the wares of the vendor across the lane. She fondled a few peaches, rolled plums between her fingers and suggestively grasped a cucumber.

"I had an idea for a fruit salsa," she called to Errol.

"It was good running into you, Taryn." Errol reached out to touch her hand, but she recoiled.

Politeness required her to say the same, but she couldn't quite manage it. She nodded and threw on what she knew was a stupid grin.

"Taryn!"

Taryn turned as she heard her brother's cry through the crowd.

"Taryn!"

She saw him weaving through the crowd and waved him over. "Bobby, what are...?"

Panting, he stopped in front of her and leaned both hands on his knees as he fought to catch his breath. "Mom... You gotta come..."

"What? Bobby, what are you saying? What happened?"

"Mom... fell... hospital."

Taryn felt the ground fall out from under her. The fatigue of the past days caught up with her, strangled her and kept her from breathing as she should. The bag of grapefruits and pineapples slipped through her fingers and fell to the ground. As the grapefruits rolled off, she stared blindly at her brother trying to make sense of what he was saying. The stalls around her spun like a tornado of confusion.

"Taryn," Errol said as he put a hand to her shoulder. "You okay?"

She nodded and pulled away from him, though clearly she was not okay.

"Come on," Bobby said. "One of us has to go to the hospital and the other has to go back to the restaurant."

The world was crashing in around her and she didn't have the strength to resist the pull of the ground as she crumbled.

"Taryn!" Bobby grabbed her arm, but was unable to keep her from hitting the ground.

"I have her," Errol was quick to say as he grabbed her other arm.

"I'm fine," Taryn muttered in weak protest.

"Stop arguing. You're far from fine." He swept her up into his arms, while Bobby still held her hand.

"Hey, I don't know who you think you are, sir..." Bobby hesitated as he scrutinized Errol's face. A vague hint of recognition crossed his gaze. "This is my sister. I'll take care..."

"Errol," Suzanne said as she returned to Errol's side. "What's going on?"

"Pick up whatever you think you need and get back to the restaurant."

"But I thought we were..."

"You can handle this on your own, Suzanne."

Through the fog and haze of her confused mind, Taryn smiled and felt a moment of victory.

"My friend is having a difficult moment and I'll tend to her."

Victory faded and was replaced by a sharp stinging sensation. *Friend?*

"I have complete faith in you, Suzanne. I'll call you to give last minute instructions for tonight's special dinner, but I know you can pull it off."

Taryn wanted to groan her disenchantment.

"Let's get you home," Errol murmured to Taryn as he carried her to his car.

Chapter 5

"We're only live a few blocks away." Taryn's brother pointed up the street.

Errol opened the passenger door and settled Taryn in the seat while gesturing to her brother to get in the back.

"Take Lyon up to Parker and take a left then right on Glebe."

Errol followed the directions and smiled as he imagined Taryn growing up in this neighborhood.

"Now take a right on Zerega and left on Frisby. It's just down there… the door where that yellow Hummer is parked."

Errol managed to find a parking space a few doors down from Taryn' home and carried her up the stairs. The building looked like it'd seen a few decades pass by, but it was well kept and clean.

"I can take it from here," the younger man said.

"What's your name, son?" Errol set Taryn on the couch in the small, but tidy living room. He sat on the edge of the couch and looked up at him.

"Bobby," he said with an indignant cock of his brow. "And you're..."

"Errol. Errol King."

A quirky and crooked grin came to Bobby's lips. "Yeah, that's what I thought. So you're her..." He pointed to Taryn. "Her... teacher?"

Errol chuckled at the implied question, but refused to address it. "I don't think Taryn will be able to go to the hospital or the restaurant."

"Yeah. Um." Bobby patted his thighs with indecision. "I gotta get a few of my mom's things. I have no idea how long they're going to keep her."

"Where is she?"

"Pelham Bay."

"Gotta car?"

He shook his head. "In the panic of the moment, I just rushed out of the restaurant and headed to the market. It's actually faster by foot than by car, what with all the one ways and the traffic. Besides, I hadn't thought far enough to think we'd come here."

Pulling the car keys out of his pocket, Errol held them out to Bobby. "Look, take the car. Leave me the things that Taryn bought for the restaurant and bring what you need to your mother."

"But there's nobody running the restaurant." He looked at his watch. "We have about only a few hours before the dinner rush starts."

"I'll take care of it."

"Sam's isn't one of your fancy…"

"I said, I'll take care of it."

Dumbfounded, Bobby headed to his mother's room and Errol brought his full attention to Taryn. As he'd spoken to Bobby his hand had gently played with the wisps of hair that played at her brow.

Her eyes fluttered open and a faint smile came to her lips.

"How you feeling, Princess?"

She looked at him as a single tear trickled down the side of her face.

"Don't worry." He took her hand and kissed her palm. "Everything's under control. You're exhausted, Taryn. You just need to rest."

A knock sounded at the door and Bobby rushed back into the living room to answer. "Hey, man. Good to see you."

Matt came in, heroic in his FDNY blues, and tall, handsome and concerned. Concern, however, turned to suspicion when he saw Errol.

"Taryn," Matt said after a curt nod to Errol.

She propped herself up on one elbow and looked at him. "Matt, what are you doing here?"

"I wanted to know if there was anything I could do to help."

"I'm going to go finish packing Mom's things," Bobby interjected as he left them.

Taryn nodded, but kept her gaze on Matt. "But… How d'you know?"

"I was there when your mother fell." He headed into the kitchen, opened the freezer and popped a few ice cubes into a glass which he then filled with lemonade.

He was obviously at ease and comfortable in the Cummings household, and Errol couldn't help but wonder how often he'd come to see Taryn.

Matt returned and handed Taryn the glass, all while adeptly ignoring Errol. "You're pale and probably dehydrated. Drink this."

Taryn struggled to sit up. "Thanks, Matt."

The beaming smile she shined onto Matt infuriated Errol and he soon realized he'd tightened his grip on Taryn's hand.

She pulled her hand free of his and fixed her gaze on Matt. " Mom. Where is she? Who's at the restaurant? What's going to…"

"Hush, Taryn." Errol tried to regain control of the situation that was quickly slipping through his fingers. "Bobby's taking what your mother needs to the hospital and I'll head to the restaurant as soon as you're settled in."

***

Taryn looked at Errol in amazement. What could he possibly be thinking? What had happened to Suzanne? What was he doing here? In her house? The haze of the past moments wore off and she looked at her surroundings with a fresh eye.

"No, Errol. I'm fine. I want to know what happened. I want to know where my mother is." She looked at Matt for an answer.

"She wanted to change a light bulb in the kitchen. I guess she was in a hurry and didn't set up the ladder properly. It collapsed under her and she fell. From what I could gather, she hit the counter first then landed hard on the floor. I was way out in the dining room and I heard the thud."

"Was she conscious? Is she all right?"

"She was conscious, but in pain."

Bobby emerged with his mother's little green suitcase. "I'm going to head out there now."

"I want to go with you, Bobby," Taryn said.

"Taryn, you had a nasty fall yourself," Errol reminded her.

"I didn't fall," she argued. "I just had a moment of weakness. I have to go, Errol." The heat of tears burned on her lower lids.

"Not that I don't' want you to come, Taryn," Bobby said, "but someone has to go to the restaurant."

"I said I'd take care of that," Errol repeated.

Taryn sat up, forcing Errol to stand. "What do you mean, take care of it, Errol? This is my restaurant and I have a dinner crowd coming in. I have dishes to prepare, people to guide and..." She quickly realized she'd sat up too fast and felt the room spin.

"You seem to forget that I have a restaurant... several, as a matter of fact. I'm well aware of the in's and outs of dealing with a dinner crowd. I'll prepare your dishes and will guide your employees."

"No, Errol. You don't understand. The people at the restaurant aren't chefs. They're not even sous-chefs. They're assistants. They do what I say. Me and my mother and Bobby do most of the actual cooking. Without us there..."

"I'll bring in some of my people."

The room remained in stunned silence for a strained moment. Matt stared suspiciously at Errol, while Bobby barely contained his obvious admiration for the world class chef.

Taryn simply wondered what he was up to.

"Let me do this," Errol said softly as he looked directly at Taryn.

She looked at him for a long, hard moment. She didn't really have much choice. She and Bobby both wanted to be with their mother. Someone had to go to the restaurant. "All right," she said.

"I'll drive you two to the hospital then head to the restaurant," Errol said.

"I can take them to the hospital," Matt offered.

Errol turned to him with a determined scowl. "I said I'll take them." He held his hand out to Bobby who returned the car keys then looked at Taryn. "Come on."

***

"So, what's the deal with this Errol guy?" Bobby asked.

They'd been sitting in the waiting room for over an hour. A nurse had assured them their mother was fine and would be back in her room after a small series of tests.

"Well, I'm sure you recognize that he's Errol King, the chef. That's why he was so adamant about helping with the restaurant." She bit her lip and wondered if she should call him to make sure everything was running smoothly.

Bobby shot her a mocking gaze. "Really? That's why? Not because something's going on between you two?"

"He was my teacher back in Paris, but you already know that."

"Yes, what I don't know is what happened outside the classroom."

"You're inventing stories again, Bobby."

"You're avoiding the obvious. That guy's into you."

"Your adolescent mind is taking over."

"Why are you denying it, Taryn? Don't you think I can tell? I mean, a guy can tell when another guy has the hots for a girl, that is unless he's really, really discreet, which this guy wasn't. I mean, it was written all over his face. He wants you. He wants you bad. He wants you in that silly way a guy will do anything to please a girl."

Taryn inhaled deeply and tried to look annoyed, but the little girl deep inside her thrilled at the notion that he'd notice how much Errol wanted her. She wanted to clasp his hand and say, really? You really think he likes me?

"Is he the reason you left Paris all of a sudden?"

She looked down the hall to see if a nurse or doctor wasn't on the way to update them on their mother's status.

"You don't have to answer. I can see it in your eyes, even if you do try to turn away. You know, I might be younger than you, Taryn, but I'm old enough to know you shouldn't throw away your dreams and ambitions because of some guy." He wrapped his arms around her shoulder and tugged her to him. "So, what'd the guy do? Make a promise he didn't keep? Lead you on and leave you hanging? Tell you he loves you then cheat on you?"

"Drop it, Bobby?"

He gasped with realization. "You fell in love with him, didn't you?"

"You're being absurd."

"He is a really handsome guy… suave and debonair and all that crap. I mean, even I can tell that. And he seemed nice enough. A little bossy, maybe, but, hell, he's at the restaurant right now so we can both be here together with our mother. You gotta give a guy credit for that."

Taryn smirked at her brother's admiration for Errol. To classify him as 'nice enough' and just 'a little bossy' was an amusing notion.

"But no matter how nice he might be, if he's out here to hurt you, he'll have me to contend with."

A nurse quietly came up to Taryn's side. "Taryn and Bobby Cummings?"

"Yes," they both said as they shot out of their chairs.

"Your mother is just coming out of her MRI. You'll have a chance to see her for a few moments before she goes on for the CT scan. She might be a bit groggy. We had to give her something for the pain."

"Can you tell us anything about her condition?"

"She appears to have a dislocated hip, the major source of her pain, and we're checking to make sure she doesn't have a concussion. Doctor Willix should be able to tell you more."

She backed away just as their mother was wheeled into the corridor.

"Mom," Taryn said as she rushed to her side and took her hand. "Mom, we're here."

Samantha pressed a tight grin and looked from Taryn to Bobby and back again. "Silly me," she murmured.

"It was an accident, Mom. Don't worry about it. Everything's under control."

"I fell," she went on, shaking her head. "The ladder wobbled, but I went up anyway and I fell."

"Yes, you fell, but you're being taken care of, Mom."

"I love you, Mom," Bobby threw in, obviously overwhelmed by the sight of his mother in such a state.

"Sorry, but I've got to get her to her CT."

"Yeah," Taryn muttered. "Of course. We'll be right here when you come out, Mom."

Standing side by side, Bobby and Taryn kept their eyes on their mother until they could see her no more. Taryn extended her fingers out to reach for Bobby's. She wanted to crumble, and fall, and cry into his shoulder. She wanted to abandon the tough exterior she fought to maintain in order to be strong for her little brother. She'd fallen once. She didn't want to let it happen again.

Bobby looked at his watch.

"You gotta get to school, don't you?" Taryn said.

With his lips pressed into a grim line, he looked in the direction their mother had gone, and nodded.

"You go ahead, Bobby. I'll stay here with her. There's nothing you can do anyway."

"But…"

"You know she'll be mad as hell if she finds out you missed a class because of her."

He snorted. "Yeah, I guess." He shoved his hands in his jean pockets. "You gonna be okay here alone?"

"Sure. Besides, if I start feeling dizzy again or something, hey, I'm already at the hospital."

"Forever the pragmatic."

The sting of tears quickly burned her eyes as she heard her mother's words repeated by her brother.

"Yeah, I guess that's me; pragmatic."

Bobby put his hand to her shoulder. "Call me if there's anything… even if I'm in class. I'll let my teacher know about the situation so I can take the call, no matter what."

"Okay, fair enough."

He kissed her brow and walked away. "I'll be back the minute class lets out," he shot over his shoulder.

Taryn sat down and felt more alone than ever. Maybe she couldn't handle this alone, she thought. But barely five minutes after Bobby's departure, Matt arrived.

Every nurse turned to look at him and a female patient even tried to get out of her wheelchair to greet him.

He was good looking, no matter what he wore. He had that magnetism, that charming air of confidence that never ventured to the point of being pretentious or arrogant. But walking down that pale hospital corridor in that deep blue that instantly declared he was a firefighter, he was the epitome of the American hero.

"I tried to get here earlier, but…"

"Matt," Taryn cut in as she stood and allowed herself a moment of weakness and leaned into him. "I'm so glad you're here."

She could almost hear the envious murmurs of the women down the hall.

"Oh… good." He sounded relieved as he pulled her into his arms. "How's your mother?"

"They keep wheeling her from one test to another." Taryn pulled away and sat down. "They think she might have a concussion."

"Look," Matt said as he sat beside her. "I have a few hours to kill. I can stay here with you for a while."

"That'd be nice. Bobby just left and, I admit, I don't really feel like being alone right now." She looked at him, his beautiful blue eyes filled with compassion and understanding. "Did I thank you for everything you did?"

"You did."

"Well, thank you again. I hate to think what would have happened if you hadn't been at the restaurant when she fell."

He shrugged. "I'm sure someone would have brought her here."

"Probably, but not as quickly as you were able to."

Nodding, he reached out to hold her hand. "It's all part of the job."

"So, you're just being a professional." Taryn smiled and held up their joined hands.

He gave her hand an affectionate squeeze. "I've known your mother since... when? Fifth grade? Six grade?"

"Something like that. I remember you coming around to play with Bobby. Even though he was a few years younger than you, you guys had a blast together."

There was something shy and sweet about the way he looked at her. "I'm sure you realize by now that I was really going over to your house to see you. Don't tell Bobby, but he was just the excuse to get me in the house."

Taryn chuckled. "Know what? I think he knows."

"I mean, now that we're older, we're good friends, but back then... Hey, it was fun all the same."

"You're such a good guy, Matt."

He let out a wry chuckle. "Hmph... good guy."

Chapter 6

"How 'bout getting a bite to eat," Matt suggested.

Taryn looked at her watch. It was almost dinner time. She hadn't had lunch and she couldn't even remember what she'd had for breakfast. "Sounds good."

They headed to the cafeteria, grabbed a few sandwiches and went outside for some fresh air.

"You seem to be spreading yourself out pretty thin these days," Matt said as they found a shaded spot and sat down in the dry grass.

"It's only until Bobby finishes his college courses. Even though things are going well at the restaurant, we can't afford to hire right now."

"And with your mother in the hospital?"

"We'll figure it out." She shrugged and took another bite of her sandwich. Her mouth full, she smiled and waved a reprimanding finger at Matt. "And don't you dare tell me I'm pragmatic."

"I remember when you guys first went to work at that restaurant. My parents thought you guys were nuts. A woman running a restaurant alone with her two kids... and in New York. And in the Bronx to boot. Takes guts."

"I come from a long line of gutsy women. My great-grandmother, Mary Cummings, started that restaurant. It was really just a counter back then. For the longest time, all she made was sandwiches, and in the fall and winter, she'd make soup. Simple, really. My great-grandfather had gone off to war, and she was left here trying to make ends meet with six kids to feed. My mom once said it cost her something like three cents to make a sandwich that she sold for five cents. She could make a whole pot of soup for a buck twenty and she'd sell fifty bowls of soup at seven cents each."

Matt looked at her with open admiration as she told him of her family's history. "Quite a business woman."

Taryn nodded. "My grandmother, Mavis, and her sister, Charlotte, went to work there when they were twelve and thirteen. Mavis was quick with the knife and could turn out sandwiches faster than you could order them. And Charlotte had a talent for pies, so… Anyway, when my mom turned sixteen she went to work there, the place got bigger, the menu got longer and now…"

"So your culinary talent has been passed down, generation to generation."

"Really. You know, when we recently started adding new menu items, we didn't know how people would react. I mean, we were basically a deli, and here we were daring to offer a few gourmet dishes for the dinner crowd. But it caught on."

"And look at you now."

"Yeah, bigger and better than ever."

"And more exhausted than ever."

Taryn gathered the sandwich wrappings and napkins and shoved them in the plastic bag they'd carried their sandwiches in.

"You know, if there's anything I can do to help… anything." A forlorn expression came to his face as he leaned in closer.

Taryn saw the kiss coming, but remained immobile for a frozen moment. Matt was so sweet, so kind-hearted… so the type of guy her mother would love to see her get involved with.

His lips were soft and warm, and in that hesitant kiss, Taryn felt all the yearnings of all those years he'd had a crush on her. But for her, the kiss lacked the spark, the thrill, the hungry need she'd become accustomed to with…

Damn it, she thought as she leaned into Matt. *Errol is over and done with. Move on. Matt is right there. Go for it.*

But after a brief play of their tongues, Taryn backed away. "Matt..."

He bit his lip and looked down.

"As great as it is being with you, and as wonderful as that kiss was... I just don't want to lead you on. I have too many things going on now to even think of... this. Besides, I just got out of a difficult relationship and I don't think it'd be fair to you to fall back and rely on you right now."

"I'm strong. I can handle it." He looked up at her, his gaze honest and loving.

"I know you can."

"Can I ask you something?"

"Sure."

"Is it that French chef guy who was at your place?"

She frowned. "Why would you think that?"

Savor Me (The Master Chefs Series #2)

"Because the guy looked like he wanted to toss me out the window the moment I walked in." He chuckled. "I think he would have if you hadn't been right there."

"Errol and I a... were close. He was my teacher; my mentor." She almost slipped and used the present tense instead of past tense.

"Look," Matt said. "I'm not going to press you for more information. I mean, it's really none of my business anyway, but..." He smiled, but he eyes were filled with sad longing. "Whenever it all blows over and you think you might be ready for a real and meaningful relationship... one with just a normal guy like me... well... you know where to find me."

***

After the last of her tests for the day, Samantha was brought to her room and Taryn stayed at her side until

Bobby arrived from school. Seated on a chair she'd pulled up to her mother's bed, Taryn had her head on the mattress until she heard Bobby's steps coming into the room.

"How's she doing?" he whispered.

"She's been sleeping for the past hour or so." With a deep yawn and a much needed stretch, she added, "I kinda dozed off, too."

Bobby came around and kissed his mother on the forehead then looked at Taryn. "I hope it did you some good. You ready to go to work?"

"Yeah, I guess. Any news on how things are going?"

"I'm almost afraid to find out."

Taryn got up and leaned over her mother. "We're going to the restaurant now, Mom," she whispered into her mother's ear. "We'll be back first thing tomorrow morning. I love you."

Bobby drove their mother's SUV all while describing the lessons he'd learned that day. Taryn was proud of him and enjoyed seeing the rapture in his eyes when he spoke of his future with the restaurant. As a handsome young man, he could have chosen so many other professions.

"How'd you get to school? I thought you'd left your car at the restaurant."

"Cab," he said simply.

Minutes later he pulled up in front of Sam's.

"Ready for a catastrophe?" Bobby said.

"Errol is a word class chef, Bobby. You're grossly underestimating him."

"Yeah. Grossly. He doesn't know our way of running things."

Taryn simply laughed as she opened the door to the kitchen. The familiar clang of pots and pans, and clink of dishes and bowls filled the kitchen, along with the sizzle and scent of good food.

Errol was in full control, doling out orders to the appropriate employee. She also noticed a few unfamiliar faces.

"Taryn. Bobby. You're back." Errol was completely at ease. To anyone else who might enter the kitchen, it was his restaurant.

"You seem to have everything under control."

"Did you expect anything less?" His grin was playful and flirty.

"Of course not."

"Well then, my fair lady…" He made a dramatic gesture of taking off his apron and passing it over her head. "I humbly return to you the reign of your kingdom."

For a moment, Taryn was dumbfounded. Errol stood before her, as if waiting for her directions.

"Are you sticking around?"

"Why not? It's too late for me to return to La Benicoise now, so I may as well finish what I started here. Besides, I can bring you abreast to all that's been happening and needs to happen."

"Perfect. Fine. Good." In truth she was a little nervous about running her restaurant right in front of him... of doling out commands to her teacher and lov...

"The floor is yours." With an elegant flourish, he bowed.

Taryn snapped out of her momentary haze, addressed her staff, introduced herself to Errol's sous chefs and took the reins. After a few orders, she got back in the swing of things and almost forgot Errol was there. On a few occasions, she even gave him a direct command, commands that showed nothing of their prior personal relationship.

Professional and quick, Errol did as he was told without question and with unerring precision. Several times, he even foresaw her needs and prepared items before she asked for them.

"Arnie," she called out. "There's a mess at table six."

Juggling chopping an array of vegetables, peeling potatoes and rinsing lettuce, Arnie looked up with a 'are you kidding me?' expression.

"I'm sorry. I have no one else to send out. There's coffee all over the floor and I have to have it cleaned up before someone slips and sues the pants off me."

"I'll go."

With three orders in one hand and two plates in the other, Taryn turned to Errol. "You? Errol, what are people going to think if they see Errol King mopping the floor?"

"They can think what they like," he said as he leaned in close to her. He winked and backed away to reach for the mop propped up in the corner. "Table six, you said?"

She nodded and stared at him for a mind-numbing moment. He was being so sweet... too sweet. Something had changed about him. He wasn't the same Errol she'd come to know in Paris. He was gentler, kinder, more patient... more giving. Maybe it was the New York air.

Maybe it was... no. She instantly silenced the optimistic thought and returned to work.

An hour later, the dinner rush subsided and they maintained a calm but functional pace for the remainder of the evening. After Taryn had had a chance to declare her undying gratitude for their help, Errol dismissed his sous chefs.

As Taryn personally took care of the finishing touch on her seafood pasta dish, she saw Errol by the stove with Bobby. A patron had asked for a steak ... well done.

"Some people think well-done means it should slap this counter the way the sole of a shoe would."

"That's pretty much the way I've seen it," Bobby said.

"Properly cooking a well-done steak is an art form in it of itself. Here…" Errol picked up a pan.

Taryn had had plenty of opportunities to see Errol's manners when it came to teaching. He could be rough, sometimes demeaning, at others downright condescending. Yet, here he was with Bobby, just two guys exchanging notes over a grill.

She'd never seen that smile on Errol before; a smile that lacked sexual innuendo, mockery, or self-appraisal. A smile that was just pure enjoyment.

Chapter 7

Taryn pulled off her apron and tossed it on the counter. "What a night."

Errol leaned against the counter across from her and folded his arms against his chest. "You were an impressive sight to see. Back at the institute you'd given the impression you didn't know how to run a restaurant…"

"Not that I couldn't run a restaurant, I just didn't think I did it as efficiently as I could. I wanted to learn better techniques… everything."

"Well, from what I saw tonight, you could give a lot of restaurant owners a few lessons."

She chuckled and noticed Bobby reaching for his jacket by the door. "Hey, where you off to? I need a ride."

"I was hoping I could skip out a little early." He looked at his watch. "I got tickets to see a show and it starts at ten."

Taryn looked at her watch. It was a quarter to. "A show, huh?" she muttered with skepticism.

"Yeah, these hip hop guys who are only in town for the weekend."

Looking at Errol, she suspected he had something to do with Bobby's night out.

With an innocent bat of his lashes, he shrugged. "I can take you home."

I'm sure you can. She turned to Bobby. "All right. Have fun, but don't stay out too late if you want to come to the hospital with me tomorrow morning."

"No matter what, wake me," he ordered and was out the door.

"You ready to go home?" Errol said. There was something familiar and cozy in the way he said it, as if they'd been going home together for so long; as if they were in the habit of ending a long, tired night together.

"I just have to sweep up the dining room and mop up here."

Errol went in search of the mop and broom, brought them back and set both upright in front of Taryn. "Pick a handle... any handle."

Her eyes met his. His gaze was playful and fun, and full of mischief. Without looking down, she reached for a handle, and Errol took the other. They both looked down.

"Looks like I'll be sweeping the dining room," Errol said.

"Fair enough."

"I'll meet you back here in five minutes." He leaned in and kissed her. It wasn't the slow, hesitant kiss of a potential lover, nor was it the deep, passionate kiss of an habitual sex partner. It was a loving peck on the lips that promised more than just a hot night in bed.

As he walked away, Taryn shook off the effect of the kiss and concentrated on the task at hand. Five minutes later he returned and put the broom away. He leaned against the counter and watched Taryn finish with the mop.

"Reminds me of my first jobs in a restaurant," he said.

"I bet it's been a long time since you mopped or swept anything."

He shrugged. "Yeah, but I admit it's something I like doing every once in a while. Don't tell the press, but I do mop up my own floors from time to time."

"With all the employees you have, why?"

Running his hand over the smooth surface of the counter, he said, "I don't know. Brings me back, I guess. It's also a weird way of reconnecting with my restaurants. Funny the things you find when you get in there and mop the floor... things like a chipped ceramic tile, a scratched table leg or a tear on a seat cushion."

Taryn chuckle. "Yeah, I know what you mean. In my case, though, I know all too well about the chipped tile and torn cushion. Right now, however, there's nothing I can do about it."

"You'll get there. I have no doubts about that."

"Thanks. Despite everything, that means a lot coming from you."

His chuckle was filled with humility as he rolled his tongue in his cheek and looked up at the ceiling as if seeking a solution to a problem.

For a moment, Taryn thought he was going to flippantly comment on her remark, but he shook his head.

"Did I ever tell you it took me three years just to break even with my first restaurant?"

"No, but I'm not surprised." Taryn finished with the mop, put it away and came to lean on the counter across from him and looked at him. "Did you ever think of giving up?"

"On a few lonely nights when I was tired of being broke, yeah, I thought about it. But then I'd get in that kitchen again, and... I'd just lose myself. Truth was, money or not, profit or not, I loved doing what I was doing."

"You're the real rags to riches story; the typical American success story."

He nodded. "You know, the first time I got a good review, I mean, the critics raved about the newest, hottest place to eat in New York... Hmph, I think I bought two dozen copies of that paper that day. I clipped out four of them. One I mailed to my Nana and the other three I framed; one went in the kitchen of the restaurant, and the other in the dining room where everyone could see. The other one I put up in my kitchen at home... if you could call that a kitchen. It was a three foot counter with a rusty old sink, a mini fridge that barely kept anything cold and a stove with only one working burner."

"Do you resent your beginnings?"

There had been only a few times since she'd known him that he'd opened up and talked of his past. Those moments were always brief, and seemingly thwart with anguish.

"Sometimes." He looked pointedly at her. "You resent anything about your childhood?"

Taryn gaped a moment, then pressed her lips together. She hadn't expected the conversation to turn to her. "Not really."

He shot her a mocking grin. "That's definitive."

"Well... resent... not really. I mean, obviously I would have preferred it if my father had stuck around... but then again..."

"Did that make you want to work harder to have control over your life?"

"Hmmm, I never thought of it that way."

"I spent the first part of my life with no control at all."

"Few of us have much control when we're young," Taryn said, trying to deny where he was going.

His eyes darkened suddenly, and she knew he'd gone to a dark place. "Maybe you're right, but at least when you have a home to go to, a bed to sleep in, and meals to fill your belly, you feel secure, safe. Just knowing that someone loves you and looks out for you gives you a certain sense of control, even if it's limited."

"All right. I'll give you that."

"Do you know what it's like to be afraid, Taryn... to really be afraid? Not the kind of fear you feel at Halloween, or when you watch a scary movie, or when you see a spider in your room, but the fear of being smacked in the head by a drunk foster dick who just likes smacking little kids for the hell of it... because he can. You run away thinking it'll be easier, better. Then you deal with the fear of roaming the streets at night with your stomach rumbling with hunger. The fear of all those strange men, winos and hobos, and bag ladies who point at you, laugh at you... want you."

"No." She shook her head, wishing there was a way of erasing all he'd been through.

"The fear that you'll be picked up by the police and brought back to the foster home that is even worse than being on the streets."

Taryn continued to slowly shake her head.

"Those years when I lived with Nana soothed that fear... a bit, but I think the hunger pangs stayed with me, even when she was filling my belly. When I got my first job at that restaurant, it was my first taste of freedom. I had some control, but it was fragile and delicate. If I made one mistake and slipped, I could lose it." He reached back for a spatula hanging on a hook and idly flipped it back and forth, as if reliving those days flipping burgers. "I think it might have made me a little obsessive. I was so damned afraid of losing what little control I'd manage to get a grip on."

Watching the play of his fingers along the spatula, Taryn felt the slow but determined welling of tears in her eyes.

"Nana gave me a bit of her savings, but I worked hard and saved every cent I could to finally open my own restaurant. Mine... sweat of my brow. There'd been days when I'd skipped meals so I could save more to open it up sooner, then more skipped meals as I tried to keep it going. Every cent mattered. Every cent was accounted for. I couldn't afford to have a waiter fuck up an order. I couldn't afford a busboy who dropped and broke dishes. I couldn't afford a girlfriend who wanted too much, who didn't understand where I was going, who would screw with my head."

"You had a lot to lose. It's understandable."

"When I got my first taste of success, and when that success went on to be solid and secured... virtually guaranteed, I couldn't let go of that control. While the media was putting up my pictures and I was being touted as the new celebrity bachelor every single female in America wanted to snag, inside I still felt like that little kid who'd wandered the streets aimlessly."

"You felt you didn't deserve your success?"

He frowned. "No. I'd worked hard. I knew I deserved it, but... I don't know. More often than not I felt like a fraud. Not the chef side of me. That I knew I owned. But the famed restaurateur, the world renowned chef, the prized bachelor... that... it didn't feel like me. It never felt like me. Don't get me wrong. For a while it was fun. I got into it. I played the game, and played it well. I controlled... everything. For all my success, I was always afraid someone would find out I was just some homeless kid who'd escaped his foster home. I was always afraid it would all go away."

"So you maintained control for your own security."

He met her gaze, his eyes filled with anguish and regret. "Obsessively."

"Do you think you'll ever be able to let go?"

"Sometimes I still have nightmares that it's all gone, but..." He nodded. "I'm here now, willing to try. I'm not saying I'm perfect, but..."

Taryn licked her lips and reached out to take his hand. His fingers instantly laced through hers and he squeezed. He let go of the spatula and reached for a dirty lock of her hair. "You're beautiful, Taryn."

She chuckled. "I'm a mess."

"You're beautiful."

For a moment, she dropped her gaze and stared at his chest. What was she to make of this confession of his? What did he want from her? What did she want from him?

Everything, a little gnawing voice said.

She met his gaze. "I want to make love to you, Errol."

He cocked his brow and his lips twisted up into a wry grin, but his grin quivered with uncertainty and his eyes gleamed with tears.

Taryn ran her hands over his chest and trailed her fingers to the nape of his neck and up through his hair. He groaned and leaned into her hands, and she felt his release. When she leaned in to kiss him, he melted into her.

"Get up," she groaned.

Obediently, he jacked himself up on the counter and Taryn quickly unfastened his pants. Considering his emotional state, she was surprised to see how hard he already was. Part of her was flattered she could get such a rise out of him while the other part questioned the validity of his story. Was he trying to pull her heartstrings? Was he just making excuses for how he'd treated her?

For the time being, she didn't care one way or the other. She wanted him. She took his erection in her hand and caressed it as Errol hissed his lack of control.

"Are you ready to release your control, Errol?"

"To you? Any time."

"Really."

"Completely."

She took him in her mouth, and as his body tensed and tightened, she knew the pleasure she brought him. His breathing was jagged, and erratic. Running his fingers through her hair, he pulled off the elastic that'd held it back, then gripped a fistful of hair as he held her close to him.

Just as she sensed he was trying to take over, trying to control the situation, she pulled back. "I'm the one driving tonight." Letting go of him, she stepped back and watched his troubled features. Disbelief, longing, disappointment, hunger and a hint of anger all played in his eyes, his lips, his hands.

Taryn ran her hands through her hair and shook it out in a wanton fashion. She pulled off her shirt and tossed it on the counter beside Errol. Her breasts heaved with every breath. It was impossible for her to hide her hunger of him, her need to have him inside her.

Errol licked his lips and watched her, his gaze interested and daring.

With a coquettish twist, she turned her back to him, kicked off her shoes and slowly pulled her pants off. She looked over her shoulder to catch his gaze. His eyes were riveted to her ass. Though she'd not had the forethought to wear a sexy and inviting thong, her snug, white cotton underwear molded to her skin in a way she knew was pleasing to the eye.

Before she could turn around to face him, Errol jumped off the counter and came to hold her from behind. His erection played along her flesh, seeking her warmth.

"You said you'd relinquish control."

"I have. You're controlling me. You're playing me like a puppet and I'm helpless," he growled into her ear. "I have no control over what you make me do." His hands came around to trail the length of her thighs and ride up to play within the confines of her panties. His fingers found the folds of skin, moist and hot, and waiting for him.

"Errol," she said with mild reprimand. "The Health Board could have my license for this."

He nibbled her ear. "I have connections. They'll let it slide." As he spoke, he tugged her panties down and deftly slid his erection inside her. Her erotic cry filled the kitchen, echoing off every wall and out of every pot and pan. She leaned over the cool counter in front of her while Errol gripped her hips and pounded into her like a man possessed.

His grunts and groans became howls and growls as the animal in him took over. Enraptured by it all, Taryn danced with him, meeting his every move.

When he finally spent himself, his orgasmic cry filling the air, he leaned over Taryn, kissed her temple and whispered. "Take me home, Taryn."

After thoroughly cleaning up, they shut the lights off, locked up the restaurant and got in Errol's car.

Without being told once where to go, he drove through the streets as if he'd been to her place a dozen times.

"You have a good memory."

"Only for the things that are important to me."

Once home, Errol followed her up without even waiting for an invitation.

"Which one is your room?" he said.

Holding his hand, she silently guided him to her bedroom. She wanted him again, for the night... all night. Decency told her that'd be impossible, but for the moment decency had little place in her heart.

Errol looked around her darkened room and smiled. "I like it here," he said. He took his time, reveling in every inch of her skin as he undressed her. When he brought her to her bed, he was gentle, patient and more giving than he'd ever been.

Whereas they'd fucked dozens of time, in dozens of positions and in dozens of places, this time he made love to her, caressing her and kissing her with an emotion that'd never been there before.

Nearly a full hour later, spent and exhausted, he lay beside her, holding her as his fingers played through her hair.

"You have to go, Errol. Bobby'll be back soon." Decency had returned.

"Let me stay." His request was soft and heartfelt. "I miss holding you… waking up to you."

"I don't want Bobby to…"

"He'll never know I'm here. I'll sneak out tomorrow morning, hours before he wakes up."

Chapter 8

Even as she slept, Taryn's skin tingled with the sensual sensations that had kept her up much of the night. Errol had made love to her, slow, soft, gentle and unbelievably giving. He'd brought her to such heights of joy and ecstasy, she was certain she'd never come back down. He'd murmured caring words in her ear, had caressed her skin with tenderness and had held her in his arms until he was ready to make love to her again.

Lying next to him, she smiled as she felt his hand on her hip and his body pressed up to her back. It was so good to be with him again, so good to feel the heat of his skin against hers.

His fingers tightened slightly as he stirred and Taryn immediately remembered where she was, sat up and looked at her bedside clock.

"Errol," she shouted as she shoved him off her. "Errol, wake up. Errol, you gotta get out of here. And I'm going to be late for work. Damn, damn, damn."

Barely opening his eyes, Errol turned onto his back, grinned and reached out to pull her to him.

"No, Errol." She shot out of bed. "I'm serious. I don't want Bobby to see you here. Get out of here before he wakes up and sees you."

Sobering slightly, he sat up, and ran his fingers through his hair. "What time is it?"

"Late. Damn it, Errol, it's too late." She cringed as she thought of Bobby's reaction should he find out about Errol.

"Don't worry." Errol got out of bed and pulled on his pants. Bleary-eyed he fumbled with the zipper while he looked around the room for the rest of his clothes. "Where's my shirt?"

Taryn tiptoed to her bedroom door and listened for signs of life. "I think you left it in the living room last night. I'll go get it."

"No." He slipped into his shoes. "Stay here. I'll grab it on the way out. Don't worry." He came up to her and pinched her chin as he winked. "I can be really quiet and discreet when I have to."

He kissed her and she realized had badly she wanted to spend the day with him, how badly she wanted to spend her life with him. She shook her head, grabbed his arm and prepared to shove him out the door. "Bye, Errol." She cracked the door enough to peek in the hall, concluded that the coast was clear and opened the door wide to shove Errol out. "Hurry."

The moment she closed the doors behind him she scrabbled to get dressed. She hopped into a pair of jeans and was reaching for her shirt when she heard voices in the hall.

Closing her eyes, she muttered, "No, no, no." She tiptoed to her door and pressed her ear to the hollow wood.

"I, uh. Last night I..." Errol stammered.

"Look, Taryn has been through a lot lately and, don't get me wrong, she's a strong girl and can take a lot of shit, but with our mother in the hospital, she's a little more vulnerable than she usually would be."

"I have no intention of taking advantage of that vulnerability."

"Really? You just walked out of that room and you're going to tell me that you didn't take advantage of her?"

"You don't understand, Bobby. Taryn and I..."

"Hey, man, maybe I didn't spend any time in Paris and stuff, but I'm a guy. I know what we do when we get a girl alone in her room."

"Hey, Bobby," Taryn said as she popped out of her room and looked at the two men in her life. Bobby, in his lucky Santa Claus boxers and tube socks, and Errol, with the unbuckled belt of his pants hanging to the side and his shirt buttoned up crooked.

"Taryn, you okay?" Bobby said.

"Of course, I'm okay, Bobby. What do you think?"

"Well, you know how it is, Taryn. This guy comes in here all cool, and smooth, and sophisticated and stuff. I know how guys can be. I know how guys who look like him can be with girls like you."

"Girls like me?"

"Yeah, you know. Like innocent and stuff. I mean, I know you ain't no virgin or anything, but…"

"Damn it, Bobby!"

Wide eyed, Bobby glanced apologetically at Errol. "What? You didn't know?"

"Bobby!" Incensed, Taryn slapped her brother's arm. "Just shut up already."

"Look, I'm just saying that I know guys. I know how they can be. Trust me."

Taryn glared at him. "Really, Bobby? Don't you think I know how guys can be, too?"

"Not the way I do."

"Bobby, stop it. You're talking nonsense."

"I'm your brother, Taryn."

"I know that."

"I'm the man of the house."

She glared at him.

"You know I'm just looking out for you, Taryn. What kind of brother would I be if I let some guy walk out of your bedroom without giving him a bit of a hard time?"

"I know, and I appreciate it, but stop it." She looked down at his state of undress. "And what are you doing up so early anyway? Didn't you come home in the middle of the night or something?"

"Actually, I just got up to go to the john and bumped into your Romeo here."

"Great. Well, now that you're up, what are you doing this morning? Are you coming in to give me a hand, or what?"

"I can't."

She cocked a cynical brow. "Hangover?"

He glared at her then grinned. "No, I do not have a hangover. I know how to hold my liquor. Actually, I have a project I have to do for school."

"Figures." She knew it was important for him to do well in school, but she desperately needed a hand at Sam's. "Happy for you, little brother. Good luck with your project, Bobby, but I've got to get to work in half an hour."

"Want me to fix you breakfast?" Errol said.

Taryn and Bobby turned to glare at him, but an eager grin came to both their lips as they nodded.

"Perfect, just show me the way to the kitchen and I'll see what I can whip up."

"It has to be fast."

"One of my first jobs was as a short order cook. I can whip up delicious scrambled eggs like you wouldn't believe."

"Great," Taryn said. "That'll give me a chance to take a quick shower."

"And wash your hair," Bobby threw in.

She looked quizzically at him.

He shrugged. "You look a mess."

"Gee, thanks."

Bobby turned to Errol and waved him over to the kitchen. "You can't always be telling them they're beautiful. It'll go to their heads."

Errol chuckled, turned to wink at Taryn and followed Bobby to the kitchen.

Taryn grimaced, muttered a few choice words and glanced at the ceiling as she turned to head into the bathroom. "Little brothers must have been invented simply to annoy older sisters."

She took a two minute shower, including a quick shampoo, got dressed again and hurried out to the kitchen before Bobby and Errol tore each other apart. To her surprise, they seemed to be enjoying each other's company.

"You know, I made breakfast the other day for this really hot chick," Bobby was saying. "I wanted to make her French toast and I like to put a few drops of maple syrup in with the eggs, you know, give it a little kick of sweetness. Girls always love the sweet stuff."

Taryn leaned against the doorjamb and watched her smooth talking little brother.

Bobby pinched his fingers together, kissed the tips and let them flourish out for emphasis. "*Mucho delicio*, you know what I mean?"

"Yes, I can imagine." Errol grinned as he listened to Bobby, all while pouring his scrambled eggs into a hot pan.

"So the next week, I meet up with the girl again. I mean, hey, she's a hot chick and I like being with her, if you know what I mean. So, anyway, she decides to make me breakfast the next morning, which I very much deserved, if you don't mind my saying so."

"Not at all."

"So, she wants to make me a cheese and spinach omelets. Quite a feat for a girl who eats cereal for dinner, you know. So I get to the kitchen, and it smells kind of nice, kind of tasty, but then kind of weird. You know, like something isn't working right. But, hey, I'm a gentleman. I don't fuss and say anything. I just sit down and let her put a plate of her work right there in front of me."

"Of course you do." Errol worked the pan and spatula to perfection.

"But then, I bite into it, and... well, if you can imagine, spinach, cheese, egg, some onion all with maple syrup."

Errol turned to Bobby with an amused grimace on his face. "I hope you took the time to give the girl a few cooking lessons."

Bobby grinned and cocked his brow. "I'm giving her her fourth class tonight."

Taryn crossed her arms, a wistful smile on her lips as she watched the scene; two players exchanging notes.

"Do you ever, you know..." Bobby obscenely punched the air in front of him. "Give girls private lessons."

Taryn cocked her head to the side and ran her tongue accusingly over her teeth as she anticipated Errol's answer.

He poured three cups of coffee, turned off the burner then glanced up at her. "Only to girls I really like." He winked.

Bobby turned to see Taryn. "You know, I think I could learn a lot from this guy."

"I'm sure you could," Taryn droned.

"Hungry?" Errol said.

"Not really, but I have to eat something. Once I get to the restaurant I won't have time to stop and eat for eight hours... if I'm lucky."

They all sat down to a plate of scrambled eggs with tiny bits of ham thrown in.

"Good," Bobby muttered with his mouth full.

"Thanks, Errol," Taryn said. "I really appreciate it."

Errol pressed his lips together and looked at her, his eyes piercing and inquisitive. He took a bite of his eggs. "I thought I'd come in and give you a hand today."

Taryn almost choked on her eggs. "Really?"

"Is that a problem?"

"Not with me, it isn't," Bobby threw in.

"No problem," Taryn said. "That'd be great. With Mom in the hospital, I don't know how I'll manage."

"Hey, weren't you going to the hospital this morning?" Bobby said.

"Yeah, after the morning rush. Visiting hours don't start until eight. I can pass by to pick you up. Will you be here, or do you have to do your project at school?"

"I'll be here 'til about nine, but then I have to go."

"I don't think I'll be able to get out that early. Can you manage with a cab?"

"Leave him the car," Errol said. "I'll take you into work, and I'll get you to the hospital to see your mom."

Taryn and Bobby looked at each other.

"I guess it's all settled then," Bobby said. He finished his last bite, and saluted Errol. "Thanks for the great breakfast, or more like a midnight snack in my case. I'm heading back to bed for an hour or so."

Taryn glared at him until she felt Errol's hand lay over hers.

"Ready to go?"

"You sure you want to come in and help out again? I mean, your restaurant…"

"I wouldn't want to be anywhere else."

Errol spent the day at the restaurant, helping out in every way possible, even bringing a few dishes to the patrons when a waitress was overloaded. When the rush subsided, as promised, he brought Taryn to the hospital.

"I'll wait out here for you."

"You sure? I could be in there a while."

"Go ahead. Take your time. I have some reading to catch up on." He held up a magazine that was flipped open to an article written about him and his restaurant.

"Hmm," Taryn mused as she pushed open the door to her mother's room. "Looks interesting. See you in a bit."

"Who are you talking to, honey?"

Taryn looked at her mother. A chill ran through her as she saw her mom, the woman who'd been there for her, always strong, no matter the situation, lying in a hospital bed. "Bobby needed the car to get to school to work on a project. I got a lift to the hospital." Before Samantha could ask more questions, Taryn rifled off her own. "Did Bobby come by yet? He said he'd come this morning."

"No, not yet."

Sitting on the edge of the bed, Taryn took her mother's hand. "The nurse seems to think you might have a dislocated hip, but I wasn't able to find the doctor to speak to him. What did he tell you?"

"Nothing much. Yesterday they had me drugged and drowsy as they sent me touring the whole hospital and taking every conceivable test. So far this morning, I had breakfast and the promise of an answer to why I'm here."

"You did have a nasty fall, Mom."

"No need to remind me. I remember it perfectly. I remember getting pissed off when the light went out at the worst possible time. I remember swearing as I brought that old rickety ladder in. I remember going up that ladder telling myself, 'Samantha, this isn't a good idea.

Samantha, this piece of crap is going to fall out from under you.' I remember the very moment I realize that, yes, the damned piece of crap did fall out from under me, and I distinctly remember the bang on my head when I hit the counter and the instant pain in my hip when I hit the floor."

"I'll go out and buy a new and sturdy ladder tonight when I close up."

Samantha waved the notion away. "Regardless, I'm never going up a ladder again. How are things at the restaurant?"

"Hectic, like usual, but we managed."

"I don't want you to drive yourself sick, Taryn. I know how you can be. You work too hard, and you're too controlling. You're going to have to delegate more. If I'm in here for a while, you might even have to hire some help."

"We'll cross that bridge later, Mom. Right now I just want to know what's going on and how you're feeling."

"They told me the doctor should come around to see me in half an hour or so."

Taryn looked at her watch. "I can't stay that long, Mom."

Samantha shot her one of her knowing glances. "Don't you think I know that, honey?" She clapped her hand over Taryn's and squeezed. "Wipe that ugly frown off your face, Taryn. You'll have a crinkled forehead like your grandma Betty. I'm fine here. I'm not lonely. I'm not worried. I'm not in need of anything. Okay, a good cup of coffee would have been nice, but, hey, I guess I'm jittery enough as it is."

"I just hate seeing you like this."

"Look at it this way, sweetie. Maybe this is God's way of making sure I get a little rest before I push myself over the edge, you know what I mean? I'll rest up good, get the doctors to fix whatever it is that's broken and then I'll be back at the restaurant better than ever."

Taryn nodded.

"Now," Samantha said as she grabbed Taryn's chin and looked her in the eye. "Who were you talking to out there? Who looks interesting?"

Startled by the question, Taryn just stared at her mother.

"Do you really think you can derail my line of question with your own, honey? I invented that."

Taryn chuckled, but still didn't know what to say. "A friend."

Sam cocked a brow. "I'd gathered as much."

"He's a fellow cook... a chef. When he heard what happened to you, he offered to come to the restaurant to help out. He's really good and he's a hard worker."

"Then why isn't he at the restaurant while you're here visiting your poor old ma?"

Shrugging, Taryn offered her mom a silly grin. "I needed a ride. He has a really nice car and I wouldn't dare drive it."

"Yeah, right." Samantha scrutinized her daughter's face. "You've really grown up, haven't you? Look at you. You're such a beautiful girl. You have the beauty men crave. The kind of beauty that makes men do stupid things. I hope he's good to you, Taryn."

"Mom," Taryn droned.

"Don't 'Mom' me. I know that look, Taryn. It's a look that could end in wedded bliss or in dismal heartache. Not to put a damper on things, but in the end it actually all comes down to the same thing."

Taryn had always suspected her mother was bitter about her divorce, but had never really heard her mother talk about it much.

"Sorry, honey." She lifted her arm to show the IV. "I'm under the influence of whatever they've got pumping through my veins here."

"That's okay, Mom. Look, I can't really stay too long."

"To tell you the truth, I'm surprised to see you here at all. I can't imagine what the morning must have been like. Go. Go and take care of business. I'll be fine here. Besides, I wouldn't want you to lose interest in whoever's waiting for you out there."

Taryn kissed her mom's cheek. "I'll try to come see you tonight."

Before Taryn could leave, Samantha grabbed her wrist. "I appreciate it, honey, and I know you mean well, but you're going to have a lot to take care of in the days to come. I don't know how long I'll be here, and even when I get out, they tell me it could be a while before I get back on my feet. I don't want you to run yourself ragged."

"I'm not, Mom, I'm…"

"I love you, honey, and I'm always happy to see you, but I don't need you to come here morning, noon and night. Work will keep you busy enough, and you're going to need plenty of rest. In between that, have some fun, honey." She patted her daughter's cheek. "You're growing too serious."

"You think?"

"I don't think; I know."

"Fine. I'll come back tomorrow."

Samantha glared at her.

"Or the day after that." Taryn backed away and waved at her mom. "Just promise you'll call to let me know how you're doing."

"Deal."

Taryn walked out and quietly closed the door. Her gaze cast to the floor, she felt Errol's presence beside her.

"You okay?" He set his hand on her shoulder.

"Yeah, fine." She looked up at him and realized her vision was blurred with tears.

"You sure?"

She shrugged. "I've just never seen my mom on her back like that. In fact, I can't remember ever seeing her lying down."

Speechless, Errol just stood beside her.

"She's strong, though. I know that. I know she'll be all right. I'm just a little rattled, that's all." She looked up at him. "We better hurry back to the restaurant."

Their return to the restaurant was a few minutes short of disaster as patrons entered for their noonday meal, but no one was there to cook anything. Errol and Taryn threw themselves into the frenzy, making up for lost time and churning out dish after dish.

Even with the frenzied pace, Errol never neglected to plate the dishes properly, ensuring each dish looked as good as it tasted. They barely had a half hour's lull before the rush for dinner began.

Hours later, exhausted, sweating and hungry, Taryn pulled off her apron. "For a minute there, I thought I was going to lose it." She wiped the sweat off her brow and leaned back against the counter.

"Tomorrow I'll bring in people from Benicoise again."

"Don't be ridiculous, Errol. You need them at your restaurant."

"Then what do you propose to do?"

"I don't know. Maybe I'll have to hire someone."

"You said so yourself; you can't afford it."

"I'll figure it out."

"All right. Come on then. Let's clean up and I'll bring you home. I can help you figure it out later."

Twenty minutes later, he pulled up in front of her home. As she opened the door, she realized he'd not made a move to come up. "Are you com...?" She stopped herself. The night she'd spent with him had been great, but it didn't mean anything. It couldn't mean anything. With everything that was going on in her life, she couldn't afford to sink herself in a relationship that was doomed.

"I have to stop by my restaurant to make sure everything went well."

"Of course. You've been neglecting your duties." She tried to hide her disappointment. Throughout the busy and hectic day, thoughts of him had sprung into her mind, sometimes at the most inopportune times. His hands on her thigh, his lips at the small of her back, his tongue behind her ear. Regardless of how she felt about their doomed relationship, damn if she didn't want him more than anything else.

"I'll only be fifteen minutes or so. Can I stop by after?"

A giddy smile made it to her lips before she could stop it. "Sure."

Chapter 9

The hectic rush of the weekend had come and gone. With Bobby off from school, he was able to give a worthwhile helping hand at Sam's, but with the endless weekend crowds, it barely showed.

By Sunday night, Taryn was pale and felt even paler. She didn't want to complain and didn't want to whine, but somewhere, deep inside her, a little girl was crying for her mommy. She wanted to cuddle up in bed and not wake up for the next twenty-four hours.

"How you holding up?" Errol seemed to have an annoyingly endless well of strength and energy, and while Taryn greatly appreciated all the energy he brought to her little restaurant, she couldn't help but wonder where it all came from.

He'd made love to her every night for the past week, and spent endless hours helping Bobby with his project, had put tireless hours at Sam's and even stopped into La Benicoise now and then.

"You make me sick," she muttered.

"Now, that's not a very nice thing to say to the guy who's been helping you out all week," he chastised.

"How can you be so peppy and full of life when I just feel like dropping into a pillow never to wake up again?"

"I don't know. Hyper active energy… adrenaline."

Taryn let her soiled apron fall to the floor as she plopped down on a stool. She teetered precariously to one side before regaining her balance.

Errol steadying her with a firm hand on her shoulder. He held his car keys out in front of her. "Here, go lie down in the car."

"I can't do that, Errol. I still have to clean up the place."

"Go lie down in the car before you fall flat on your face. I don't think your mother would like to hear that you're in the hospital room next to hers."

With a determined boost of energy, Taryn hopped off the stool and stood her ground. "I'll hurry up and clean the dining room."

Errol grasped her shoulders and gave her a gentle shake. "Taryn, you're about two minutes shy of dropping dead on your feet from sheer exhaustion. Seriously, go lie down and close your eyes. I'll clean up in here and be out in a minute to bring you home."

She looked up at him, wanting so badly to argue with him, wanting so desperately to be strong and show him that she was capable of dealing with everything around her, but her lids were heavy and her legs unsteady.

"Come." He took a hold of her upper arm, and guided her out to his car. With a quick peck on her brow, he leaned the seat back as far as it would go. "Back in a minute."

Taryn fought the encroaching sleep. Her head tilted heavily to the side and she jolted back to wakefulness. Just let go, she told herself. *For a minute, stop trying to control everything and just let go.*

Sleep came, blissful and deep. From a distance she was vaguely aware of Errol's return. He started the engine and the gentle rumbling and soft purr lulled Taryn even deeper into her slumber.

When the car came to a stop, she lifted an eyelid long enough to see Errol opening her car door.

"Come, my princess. Let's get you into bed."

He lifted her out of the car and she instantly cuddled into him, finding sleep again as she pressed her face into the crook of his neck. Only when she heard a strange and unfamiliar rumbling and felt an odd stirring in her gut did she awaken.

"Where are we? Errol, where are you taking me?" She looked around the small and dimly lit cubicle; an elevator.

Before Errol could answer, the doors slid open and he entered his penthouse apartment. "I'm bringing you where you can get a good night's sleep; where you can relax, forget about the day, forget about tomorrow and just enjoy the night." He set her down on her feet.

Mesmerized she looked around her. The apartment was sparsely, but richly furnished and was strictly in wood tones, black and white. Large windows looked over Manhattan and in the distance she could see the sparkling lights of the Brooklyn Bridge.

"Errol, with everything I have going on, I can't waste time coming to your place."

"Rejuvenation is never a waste of time." He pulled her shirt up over her head and reached around to unclasp her bra.

She looked at him, her body at once aroused, but also physically exhausted. "Errol, I don't think I'm up to…"

"Hush. Get your mind out of the gutter for once." He winked and threw on a cocky grin as he pulled off her shoes and socks, then rid her of her jeans and panties.

Standing totally nude before him, her skin tingled with anticipation.

He took her hand and led her into the bathroom.

Gaping, she couldn't help but be awed by the beauty of the room. Larger than her living room at home, expensive and exotic tiles covered the floor while a smaller version of the same tiles ran up the wall giving the entire room an air of quiet elegance and rich opulence.

Errol ran a bath, added scented oils to the gurgling water then turned to the sound system cleverly hidden in an antique armoire. With a flick of a switch, the slow melodic plucking of a blues guitar filled the air.

"You haven't had a decent bite to eat since that long ago breakfast. Soak up the warmth, breath in the sweet scents and lose yourself in some of the best blues this side of Memphis. I'll be back in twenty minutes."

For a moment Taryn felt a tug of regret. Was he just going to leave her here… alone? But the moment she put her toe in the warm water, the moment the heated oil brought wafts of heavenly scents to her nostrils, she knew this was exactly what she needed. She sank into the water, laid back and lost herself.

When Errol returned she was in a deep state of relaxation.

"Don't move," he ordered. He proceeded to hand feed her chunks of pineapple, mango, and whole strawberries dipped in deep, dark chocolate. "Fresh fruit is a great elixir."

"This is so good," she said as she chewed on a piece of mango. "I didn't even know I craved something so cool and refreshing."

"As much as I love to cook, as much as I love every minute I spend in my restaurant, at the end of the day, the overwhelming odor of so much food can sometimes be too much."

She looked up at him. He was so devilishly handsome, so boyishly charming and so innocently beguiling. "Why are you doing all this, Errol?"

"Doing what?"

"Bringing me to the hospital. Helping out at the restaurant. Hand feeding me strawberries."

He looked at her for a long moment. "Not many people know this, but a few years ago a good friend of mine was spending all his free time at the hospital. His son was battling leukemia and it was a very difficult time for his whole family. Every chance I had, I'd bring him to the hospital and sit with him as he waited to see his son, waited to get a word with the doctor, waited to get results from yet another test."

Keeping her eyes closed, Taryn listened to him and allowed the sound of his voice to flow over her body. His voice was soothing, sure and strong and intensified her relaxed state.

"When he started falling behind on his bills – mortgage, car, health insurance – I wrote him a check to cover it all so that he could continue to be at his son's side instead of going back to work."

Touched by his story, Taryn smiled. "That was really sweet of you," she whispered. "Loaning money to a friend can be risky."

"It wasn't a loan. I never loan people money. If I feel it's needed, I'll hand it over. If not, don't even bother asking."

"I guess that makes sense."

"Then, about a year ago, a friend found himself in a situation similar to yours. He was going nuts trying to keep up, trying to juggle so much in his life, but he just couldn't manage. I jumped in, helped him out for... what was it? Six weeks I think. Then things picked up, things started looking better for him, and he went on to be a big success."

She cracked her eyes open. "So you're just helping me out of the goodness of your heart."

"Well, that and I get to see you naked in a bath." He chuckled as he popped the last piece of pineapple into her mouth.

"Cute." She closed her eyes.

Errol set the empty platter on the counter, took Taryn by the hand and helped her stand.

"I have to come out already? This feels so good."

"I don't want to wait until you come out of there looking like a dried fruit." With a big, fluffy towel, he patted her dry and while he lingered a moment at her breasts and thighs, he didn't push the sexual aspect any further. "Besides, what I have in mind will feel even better." He led her into his bedroom and had her lie face down on his bed.

"Should I be concerned about this?" Taryn asked as she propped herself up on her elbow and looked at him.

"Trust me."

"Haven't I heard that one before?"

"Just lie down." He pushed her head down onto a small pillow. After dimming the lights, he turned some music on and came to kneel over her on the bed.

Every inch of her skin anticipated his touch. What did he have in mind now? What implement would he use to arouse her? What insane and wild technique would he try out on her?

She heard the squirt of liquid, the clap of hands then detected the light scent of vanilla.

Warm, oily hands pressed into her shoulders and Taryn let out a groan that released the stress of the day.

Errol's hands and fingers pressed over her skin, gently prodded her muscles and loosened every tightness that had built up over the past days. With exquisite pressure, he pressed his fingers down to her lower back and rolled his thumbs back up to her shoulders.

For the next twenty minutes his hands rubbed, massaged and tweaked all traces of strain away, leaving her heavy and lethargic. When he traveled over her buttocks, she thought he'd turn the relaxing massage into a sexual tryst, but his hands continued down over her thighs, down her calves and took a hold of a foot.

Tears of relief lined her closed eyes as the pain of standing all day were erased and replaced with the heavenly sensation of flying. As Errol started the same treatment on her other leg and foot, she felt the first pulling of much needed sleep.

She wanted to remain awake to feel every sensation he brought her, but sleep was too delicious, too tempting and too impossible to resist. With only a vague notion of the time that had passed she awoke to Errol's hands riding up her leg and trailing to her inner thigh.

Innocently, his fingers brushed along the delicate folds of skin at the crux of her thighs. An instant stirring of arousal shot through her. He worked his way down to her ankle and slowly trailed up her thigh, his fingers brushing once again along the now moist skin.

After several titillating passes over her legs, he brought his attention to her back. His fingers hugged her sides, reaching shyly to touch the sides of her breasts.

Taryn swallowed the ball of eroticism that filled her throat. His touch was so slow, so teasing, so innocent… it was enough to drive her crazy.

"Turn over." His command was an aroused croak.

Errol took the same slow ministrations to her legs, only now his fingers lingered over her moistened folds longer and longer. Taryn tried to control her rousing hunger, but despite her attempts, her hand snaked out to reach for the waist of his pants.

"No, no," Errol whispered. "Lie back and relax."

A sly grin came to her lips as she let him set the pace.

He brought his hands to her belly and trailed up just under her breasts, but instead of taking a hold of the aching orbs, he circled around them, driving her to new heights of anticipation and desire.

She licked her lips as he passed his fingers close to her breasts, again and again. For a full five minutes, he brought his hands to her legs, completely ignoring her breasts and the moist folds of skin that beckoned him. So hungry for him, she wanted to grab him, pull him onto her and beg him to make love to her.

Instead, she pressed her lips together and bit down on her desire.

When he brought his attention back to her breasts, she could hold back no more. "Errol." She reached out for him.

"Patience," he said in a velvety hush. He ran his fingers around each breast, circling closer and closer and closer, but stopping short of touching the aching and erect nipples.

"Errol."

"Hush." He leaned over her and looked deep into her eyes. "You're tired... exhausted. I don't want to be responsible for your collapse." With slow and calm movements, he got off the bed and carefully took off every stitch of clothes.

"Continue like that and you'll be responsible for the loss of my sanity." Taryn eyed Errol's magnificently hard body, drinking in the naked sight of him. He was so sculpted, tanned, and hard; she wanted to run her tongue all over him and feel him with her hands. All this time they'd been fucking every night, she still could not believe she was with someone as beautifully flawless like Errol. "I want you in me, right now, Errol."

He chuckled. "I know you have more control than that. You can take everything I dish out." Returning to the bed, he brought his lips to the tender skin on the side of her breast then the other.

Her nipples perked up higher and a tingling sensation between her legs exploded and became unbearable. She ran her fingers through his hair and nudged him closer, urging his lips to find a nipple, to suck until she screamed, until she burst.

Errol took a gentle grasp of her left hand and brought it over her head. With a loving gleam in his eye and a wicked twist to his grin, he brought his lips, soft and moist, over her nipple.

Letting out an enraptured sigh, she wrapped her fingers into the sheets as Errol brushed his entire body along her. She felt his hardness as it touched her thigh, and ignited a flame that only he could extinguish.

While refusing to allow her to move or participate, Errol entered and made love to her, long, slow and lovingly. He kissed and lightly sucked the tender skin of her neck, just below her ear. His hand delicately caressed every inch of her skin.

As he murmured softly into her ear, Taryn listened for the words she longed to hear, the words that she struggled to keep inside. They were on the tip of her tongue, in her heart and in her wishful thoughts.

How she loved this man. And the more she knew him, the more she fell deeper in love with him.

Chapter 10

"Where's your little helper tonight?" Bobby said as he picked up a cleaver and chopped up carrots and celery.

"You mean Errol?" Stirring a pot of béchamel, she shot him a sidelong glance. "He had to be at La Benicoise tonight. His sous-chef is down with the flu and another employee decided to go to his brother's wedding at the last minute."

"My, my. How will you manage?"

"No problem. You're here, and everyone came in tonight. I even put Arnie on extra duty. You know, he's really picking up every aspect of cooking and he's really good at everything I throw at him."

"Yeah, yeah. That's not what I meant, and you know it."

Turning off the burner, she set the pot aside and looked pointedly at him. "Then tell me, little brother, what do you mean?"

He looked her up and down. "You know."

She cocked a brow and resisted the urge to burst out laughing. "No, I don't know."

"Come on, sis. You've been spending every night with him. Don't you think I don't notice when you don't come home to sleep? And when you're not sleeping at his place, he's coming home with you. You guys have been together twenty-four seven for the past two weeks."

"You're exaggerating."

"You think? Even Mom has noticed. I mean, every time you go to the hospital to see her, he's right there with you."

"Of course he's there. You've got the car, silly. He's giving me a ride."

He set the cleaver down on the chopping block. "Okay, come clean. What's the deal with you and this guy?"

"Bobby, it's none of your business."

"I'm your brother. It is my business."

"Really? And do you tell me about everything that's going on in your life."

"For starters, that's different."

"Different how? And don't you dare tell me because I'm a girl and you're a guy."

"Absolutely because you're a girl and I'm a guy. What do you think?"

"I know for a fact that Mom didn't raise you to have such a chauvinistic point of view."

"It's not chauvinistic. It's just a fact. As a girl you need to deal with men, romance and sex differently than a guy does."

"I cannot believe you just said that."

"What? Look me straight in the eye and tell me how hot the sex is."

"I will not." She immediately averted her gaze and glanced into her pot of béchamel.

"See. You can't just come straight out and admit you're banging the guy."

"Bobby! You're my brother. I don't want to talk about that sort of thing with you."

"Why not? I'm the perfect person for you to bounce off any questions or whatever. I can give you my perspective."

"I don't need your perspective."

"Really? I bet that while you're banging the guy, you can't just enjoy it for what it is. You're falling in love with the guy."

"That's ridiculous."

"Is it? Last night I had a great time with Leah, a hot piece of babe. Three nights ago this tigress whose name I don't even remember, fucked my brains out. Two weeks ago I spent three nights in a row with Amber. A record for me, actually. Three nights with the same girl. But do I want more? Hell no. Do I want to talk about lovey dovey stuff? Hell no. But you... you can't help but become emotionally involved. It's in your DNA. Your heart follows your..." He glanced down at her hips. "Well, you know."

"How in the world could you be spending so much time with so many women with everything else you have going on?"

"See. Another difference. No matter how busy, no matter how tired, no matter how stressed, a guy will always find time to spill his seed."

Taryn patted his cheek. "What a romantic."

"Hey, I'm eighteen. I'll have plenty of time to fall in love and settle down to the same woman when I'm older.

For now, I just want to enjoy myself and not get bogged down by a girl who'll cry because I'm not paying enough attention to her. Take these girls in my class; Rhonda, Veronique, and Kristen. They've been all over me since day one. Okay, so I flirted a bit with them, you know, lay on the charm a bit, but before you know it, Rhonda is all jealous because I talked to Kristen for too long and Veronique is upset because I didn't call her when she insisted I call her. Girls just want too much sometimes. I mean, I got a lot to give, but there's a limit."

Taking her pot of béchamel, Taryn turned away and handed it to Arnie. "This is for the seafood pizza." She turned back to Bobby and caught his reprimanding gaze.

"You know what can happen if you let yourself fall for this guy."

"Bobby."

"You just have to prepare yourself. I mean, rich, good-looking... and a celebrity. Every woman must be dying to get close to him. You have an incredible battle ahead of you."

"No, I don't, Bobby. Nothing's going on."

"I know you, Taryn. I know when you're hiding something."

"I'm trying to hide just how annoyed I am with you at this very moment."

"Fine. Don't tell me." He put his hand to her shoulder and looked earnestly into her eyes. "All jokes aside, sis, I don't want to see you get hurt. If ever you want to talk, about anything…"

She looked up at him. He could be so young and immature sometimes, so frat boy, so party fiend, so skirt chaser… but he could also be so sweet and caring. "Thanks, Bobby. I know you mean well. I promise, if ever I want a guy's viewpoint, I'll come to you."

"Good. Glad that's settled. And while I have you in an agreeable mood, how 'bout coming to school with me tomorrow."

"Bobby, you know I can't. Between here and the hospital, I don't have time to go to a class. Tomorrow is Thursday, and we have two big deliveries coming in"

"Yes, both early in the morning. We'll have plenty of time. And this isn't just an everyday class. It's a seminar."

"Still, Bobby. You know what the Thursday rush is like."

"Not this time. Tomorrow is the Thanksgiving Parade. Remember how empty this place was last year? Everyone will be out on the streets and we won't have anyone coming in here until later. The team here can handle the few that'll trickle in before we get back here."

Taryn looked at him. Was Thanksgiving already upon them? "A seminar, huh?"

"Yeah. It's supposed to touch on everything from the newest gadgets, the hottest trends and the best business tools to use for various types of restaurants. I don't remember the speaker's name, but everyone's been talking about this seminar as not to miss. It's thirty-five bucks for non-students who want to attend, but if you come with me, you can get in free."

"Hmmm. You're right. It will be quiet here tomorrow. I guess a seminar could be interesting."

Chapter 11

Taryn hooked her hand through the crook of her brother's arm as he led her through the school he knew so well. Greeting classmates and acquaintances, he smiled and was unerringly charming. He held his head high, and seemed so proud, yet a little nervous to have her with him.

As they maneuvered their way to a seat up front, Taryn caught the few killer glares girls shot at her.

"I get the feeling I'm not really welcomed here," Taryn said. "Some of those girls literally have daggers in their eyes."

Bobby patted her hand. "I confess. That was part of the plan."

"What does that mean?"

Near the microphone set for the speaker of the day, a small group of young women chatted. A tall, lanky blonde, a shorter, curvy brunette and a plump, cupid faced blonde milled around a cute redhead. The redhead glanced up at Bobby, shot a curious gaze at Taryn and quickly returned her gaze to her friends.

"You spotted her?"

"Who?"

"Allison."

"The redhead?"

"Yeah."

"What about her?"

He tightened his hold on her. "She's the only one who hasn't succumbed to my charm."

Taryn looked at her little brother. "Bobby…"

"What?" he said with innocent wide eyes.

"Did you bring me here just to get that girl jealous?"

"Ha, what are you talking about? With all these girls constantly after me, I don't need to bring you here to make her jealous. Come. I'll introduce you."

"Fine, but I'm going to tell her that I'm your sister."

He stopped abruptly and grasped her arm. "Okay, so maybe a bit."

"But why? You just said it yourself. You've got all these girls after you. Why drag me into this? And why not just be upfront and tell this Allison girl that you like her?"

"Look, I admit it. I'm a chick magnet… no false humility there."

"Ha," Taryn let out. "False humility? There is no humility."

"So, I'm a little cocky. The girls are into it. Anyway, I attract a lot of girls, and for the most part, I have no complaints."

"But…"

"But, well, I can sometimes attract, well, let's just say, the sort of girl who doesn't have much to say."

"Ah, is my little brother maturing? Is my little brother looking for a girl he can actually converse with?"

"Look, I just think that you're a classy act, and I think Allison might look at me differently if she sees me with you."

"Classy, huh? You've never told me that before."

"I didn't want it to go to your head." He looked lovingly at her and brushed her hair off her face. "You *are* a class act, Taryn."

"Gee, thanks, Bobby. That's really sweet of you."

"See. I'm not just an ego-centric womanizer. I'm a really good guy."

Taryn patted his cheek affectionately. "I know you're a good guy, Bobby, but is this…" She waved her hand between him and her. "…all part of your attempt to get this Allison's attention?"

He flashed her a charming grin and winked. "You know me too well. Come on."

The small group of girls parted and glanced admiringly at Bobby. More deadly daggers were shot at Taryn as every girl grimaced as they swept their gaze over her.

Allison, however, smiled politely at Taryn and looked at Bobby with abject indifference.

"Hi, girls. All ready to hear the wisdom of our esteemed speaker today?"

"Hi, Bobby," the smaller dark haired girl said. "Of course we are."

"I just came by to introduce you all to Taryn."

Allison was the first to offer her hand. "Nice to meet you, Taryn. I've never seen you in class before."

"No, that's right," Taryn said. "I just came for the seminar today. I hear the speaker has a lot of interesting things to say. I run a restaurant in the Bronx and still have a lot to learn."

A tall, thin brunette came up behind Bobby and wrapped her arms possessively around his chest. "Hey, there, sweetcakes. It's about time you show up."

Bobby turned to the girl and immediately lost his grin. "Rhonda, how nice to see you."

"I thought you said you'd call me before coming. I was hoping you'd come by and pick me up."

"Well, actually, you said I'd call you before coming, but seeing how I was coming here with…" He turned to Taryn. "This is Taryn."

Rhonda's grin remained bright and joyous while her eyes took on a definitively evil glint.

Before he could answer her, the pretty blonde next to Allison stepped forward and handed him a note. "Just a little thing to keep in mind." She winked.

"Hello, everyone." A gruff, older looking man came to the microphone. He passed his fat fingers over his sweaty and balding head as he looked out at the in-coming crowd. "We have a full house today, so please move in to fill every spot."

"That's my professor, Mr. Hindley," Bobby whispered in Taryn's ear.

While all the girls turned to listen to the professor, Allison shot a sidelong glance at Bobby. Taryn caught her gaze and the girl immediately turned to look up at the professor.

"If you could all take your seats, we should be ready to start in a few moments."

Bobby sat down and three girls fought to grab the seat at his side. The shorter brunette won.

Taryn leaned into him. "So what's the deal with this Allison girl? How serious are you about her?"

"I don't know yet. Might just be idle curiosity."

"Or just the fact that she's not into you. You're turned on by the chase."

"I've had to chase girls before." He grinned. "Okay, I knew, without a doubt, that they wanted me, but still…"

"This is your first real rejection."

"Hey, hey. Be careful with that word. She hasn't rejected me. She just hasn't responded favorably yet."

Chapter 12

Mr. Hindley returned to the microphone. "We apologize for the delay. Our guest had a bit of difficulty getting around the parade in town, but... better late than never, here is, the world renowned chef you've all been waiting for... Chef Errol King."

Gaping, Taryn turned to Bobby. "Errol?"

"Yeah! Surprise!"

"Hello future chefs, restaurateurs and lovers of good food. My name is Errol King and today I want to touch on various aspects of creating innovative dishes, finding your niche and building a strong and prosperous business."

As the minutes went on, Taryn listened to Errol with a certain degree of nostalgia. She remembered her first day in class, the first words of greeting he'd spoken to the class; the first words of wisdom he'd imparted on his students.

Errol clamped his hands together and smiled as he looked out at the eager faces. Girls openly ogled him, even the girls who just moments earlier had be in complete adoration of Bobby. Guys looked at him with interest and admiration.

"I know you probably expect me to concentrate on French Cuisine, but, how about looking at something I'm sure is closer to your hearts."

"What about crème brulée?" a young man in the back called out.

"Yeah, what about the perfect bolognaise?" another complained.

"And coq au vin?"

Unfazed, Errol grinned. "Trust me. What I want to talk to you about is just as valuable, if not more valuable, than all that; the importance of local cuisine."

"What?"

"Working with the ingredients readily available to you. Working with the culture around you. Creating dishes that bring the best of what's around you and delivers it all on a plate."

As Errol spoke of the quality of ingredients available in New York and the inspiration of Parisian techniques, Taryn started to formulate her own take of a French New York dish. She thought of ways of bringing the refinement of French cuisine into the foods New Yorkers loved.

"Okay, so now," Errol said, "I invite you all to return to the kitchen stations and I challenge you to pair up and create something original, spunky and elegant. We have a little more than an hour, so let's get to work."

Taryn instantly turned to Bobby who in turn had his eyes on Allison. "You're not gonna dump me now, are you?"

Bobby turned to her. "Of course not. I have more class than that."

In the large room with dozens of cooking stations, Errol roamed around and peered over the shoulders of every pairing that were deep in secretive conversations. "I'm here if you need any technical advice, but I will not be doling out ideas, nor will I comment on the ideas you have."

Taryn caught Errol's professional glance. His lips held just the slightest hint of a knowing grin. She turned to face Bobby and leaned her head close to his. She hoped he wouldn't notice the heated blush that blossomed over her cheeks. "Before I tell you what I have in mind, do you have any ideas?"

"For now, I'm blank, so let me hear who you've got."

"Okay…"

"Once you've got your idea down, choose your ingredients and get to it."

Together, Taryn and Bobby fine-tuned their take on a French classic.

"I remember reading something about using hot spices in something like this," Bobby said.

"Spicy like what? Hot peppers? Curry? Ginger?"

"Hmmm, I think ginger could be interesting."

They worked together like a well-oiled machine. Bobby almost read her mind and she hardly needed to talk to him at all.

Taryn held the spoon up to Bobby and he leaned in to taste.

"Wow." He cocked his brow. "That's even better than I anticipated."

"Really? You're not just toying with me?"

"No, this is great. Just thicken up the sauce a bit and we're good to go."

"Good."

Within a reasonable amount of time, they put down their utensils.

Happy with the result, Taryn winked at Bobby and waited as everyone around them scrabbled to finish in the minutes that remained.

"Have you thought of a name for your innovation?" Bobby whispered into her ear.

With a pleased grin on her lips, Taryn nodded.

"All right. We've reached the end of this seminar and have only a few moments to see and taste what you've all made.

"No, this is great. Just thicken up the sauce a bit and we're good to go."

"Good."

Within a reasonable amount of time, they put down their utensils.

Happy with the result, Taryn winked at Bobby and waited as everyone around them scrabbled to finish in the minutes that remained.

"Have you thought of a name for your innovation?" Bobby whispered into her ear.

With a pleased grin on her lips, Taryn nodded.

"All right. We've reached the end of this seminar and have only a few moments to see and taste what you've all made

Errol headed to the couple closest to him. "And what have you concocted?"

"We took a French classic, crème brulée, and added a touch of New York spunk," the young girl said.

Errol picked up a small spoon, dipped it in the creamy dessert and tasted it. He pressed his lips together and frowned. "What spunk, exactly, did you add to this?"

Batting her lashes innocently, the girl looked up at him. "Pureed raspberries."

Dumbfounded, he stared at her for a stunned moment. "What part of a raspberry represents New York?"

She shrugged and looked at her partner who shrugged. "It's red and bold."

Errol patted her shoulder. "I think you need to work on it some more."

He moved on to another couple and another, and while Taryn watched him, she was surprised by the lack of venom in his remarks. He offered constructive criticism without demolishing the students or their ideas. When he came to her station, she wondered if he'd be as lenient.

Errol tasted their dish. "Interesting. Flavorful. I see New York and there's a definite touch of Paris. This is quite good."

Pleased, Taryn tried to contain her pride. "Thank you. Bobby's the one who thought of the New York side while I brought in the French aspect."

"And what would you call this creation?"

"A Taste of Errol."

He cocked a brow. "How fitting."

Nodding, he moved on. When he'd seen every new concoction, he applauded the class. "You've all shown a great deal of creativity and quite a bit of audacity. I know some of you missed the mark and your dish was less than perfect, but don't let that dissuade you from creating. All your ideas had merit. I hope you learned something from this exercise and hopefully it will serve you in the future. Everything and anything is possible. You just have to find the best way to make it work."

As the class cleared their stations and left, Taryn noticed the number of times Errol glanced at her. He seemed anxious, rubbing his hands together in a way that was so unusual for him.

"Aren't you glad you came with me?" Bobby said with a sharp nudge of his elbow in her ribs.

"Yeah, this was really a lot of fun."

He gave her a fraternal pat on the back. "It was." He glanced past her at a group of girls. "Think you can get a ride back home?"

Taryn looked at him with a stern frown. "Now you're going to dump me?"

"Come on. I've seen how you've been eyeing Errol and he's barely taken his eyes off you. You're just as eager to dump me as I am to... well not dump you, but, hey, all these girls are vying for my attention. I can't let them all down."

Grinning, Taryn looked at the eager girls waiting just outside the class. "So, who's the lucky girl?"

He shrugged. "I haven't decided yet. We'll see how things go."

"Go then." She slapped his shoulder. "Have fun."

He walked away before she'd barely finished speaking.

"Have you been left stranded?"

Crossing her arms over her chest, she turned to Errol. "Apparently Bobby has some catching up to do."

"How'd you like the seminar?"

"Interesting, but then I guess you already know that."

"I was hoping it'd be. You know, I didn't just compliment your dish because... well, because it's you. I really enjoyed it. In fact, it's unfortunate I could take just one bite."

"That's good to hear. I'll admit I was a bit nervous."

"How d'you come up with that name?"

"I don't know. I guess it's a bit of an homage to my mentor. I mean, you were in New York when you realized you wanted to be a top chef and I thought this dish represented your roots."

"I'm honored." He reached for her hand, but Taryn shot a glance around the room and pulled back when she saw a few lingering female students.

"You're not officially a student here and I'm not officially a teacher. We can fraternize, you know."

She chuckled and allowed him to take her hand. "Old habits, I guess."

He brought her fingers to his lips. "I can think of some other old habits we could maintain."

A jolt of excitement raced through her and she was instantly aroused. Once again, she glanced at the students, girls who seemed eager to speak to Errol, but who now fidgeted as they watched them.

"I think you've just disappointed a few of your fans," Taryn said.

Pulling his shoulders back into a professional stance, he released her hand and turned to address the girls. "Can I help you with anything?"

The three girls glanced at Taryn with envy and looked at Errol in dismay. Two of the girls shook their heads, waved and walked away, but the third approached him.

A hot and spicy number, her dark curls trailed down to her lower back. Between her tight and low riding jeans, and the short and frilly shirt, her midriff was daringly exposed. "You're a good cook," she said with the confidence New Yorkers were known for.

"Why, thank you."

"I was wondering if you do house calls. I would love to have you cook dinner for me some time."

"Now, that's a very interesting invitation, but it's not really something I'd do."

"Ah, well," she shot over her shoulder as she swung her hips to the exit. "Your loss."

For the first time since knowing Errol, Taryn was amused by the come on of a girl instead of threatened by it. "Looks like you broke her heart, poor thing," she said with a sarcastic grin.

"Your heart is the only one that concerns me. Come on. Let's get out of here before someone else decides to come back for something." He led her outside, but instead of heading to the parking lot, he walked toward the front curb.

"Where d'you leave your car?"

"Right here," he said as he came up to a limousine.

"You know, you don't have to try so hard to impress me, Errol. You already have my interest."

The chauffeur held the door open as they got in. "Take the long way home, Russell," Errol said.

Taryn immediately noticed the bottle of Crown Royal tucked in the bar and her party juices began to flow. Excited and giddy, she sank into the plush leather seats and gazed out the tinted window before turning her thrilled gaze to Errol. "I take back what I just said. This is really great."

"Call me lazy, but today, I wanted to concentrate entirely on you. I don't want to have to think about where to go or how to get there." He wrapped his arms around her and held her close as he looked intently into her eyes. "And I want to have both hands free for this."

Her heart swelled, filled with such intense emotions, she thought she'd burst. He was everything she could have ever wished for. Strong and enigmatic. Loving and tender. Intriguing and intelligent.

The touch of his hands on her skin not only stirred her sexual hunger, but soothed her questioning heart, and calmed her fears.

Damn it. I love you, Errol. She bit her lip to keep the words from coming out.

He kissed her, soft and tender for all of five seconds then hard and demanding. And Taryn gave back just as hard as she took. Hungry for him, she wrapped her arms around him and pressed her body to his. His hardness pressed against her and the need to taste him overwhelmed her.

She slid off the leather seat and kneeled before him. For a long moment she simply stared at him, drinking in the sight of the beautiful man he was. With a will of their own, her hands trailed up inside his pant leg, traveling over his calves and up to his thighs. His pants too tight to go any further, she was allowed only the slightest touch of his aroused member.

Errol let out a restrained hiss as his eyes hooded and Taryn let her finger ride along the length of his hardness once more before pulling her hands out. She reached out to unbuttoned his shirt down to his waist then concentrated on her own shirt. One by one, she slowly unbuttoned her blouse to reveal a delicately laced lavender bra.

Errol's gaze immediately fell to her breasts. Licking his lips, he reached out to finger the delicate lace.

While he remained entranced by her breasts, she wiggled out of her jeans. In only her bra and thong, she brought her attention back to him. With his muscular chest exposed, she leaned in to suck his nipple and occupied her hands with the removal of his pants.

"I don't believe I've ever enjoyed a ride through New York the way I'm enjoying this one," he murmured.

"And the ride has just begun." She reached into his boxer briefs and lightly ran her hand over the hardened shaft. Frowning, she looked at him with reproach. "Hmm, it doesn't look like you're very interested."

"More interested and I'd have a heart attack."

"You think? Let's check to make sure." She took a firm hold of his erection and slowly pulled up to the tip. As rigid and hard as he was, she felt a pulsation of increased arousal pump through the length of his erection.

"That's one way of checking," Errol said through labored breaths. "But how about checking with your lips, or with your tongue?"

"I'm not sure. Maybe it wouldn't change anything."

"Try," he whispered.

Taryn leaned into his crotch and kissed the soft tip of his erection. "That didn't really make much of a difference," she said with a shake of her head.

"Try again," he groaned.

She kissed the tip of his erection again, and snaked her tongue out to lick the length of his hardness.

"Am I aroused enough for you now?" Errol muttered as he sank his fingers into her hair and brought her closer.

She took him fully into her mouth and applied pressure as she pulled back. "I think I've got your interest." Her lips and tongue played over the stiff shaft as his increasingly loud groans of rapture filled the car. The sounds of his pleasure made her sucked him harder, arousing her as much as it aroused him. God, it felt good to know how much pleasure she could give him.

Just as his cries reached the threshold of ecstasy, she abruptly stopped.

"Isn't that the Empire State Building we just passed?"

"Forget that." He took a firm hold of his aching shaft. "This is the only empire you need to tend to."

"Don't you think we should take advantage of this marvelous tour? I've never seen New York quite this way." She tried to maintain an air of innocence, but knew her gaze on him was bold and daring.

"I'll tell Russell to start all over again when we're through. It'll all be even more beguiling as darkness sets in." He grasped her hips. "Now turn around and let me see your ass."

Playing with the thin strips of her thong, she turned around and leaned forward to give Errol the full view. He slapped her lightly and groaned.

"You're such a delicious slut when you want to be."

"Delicious? How can you tell?"

With a firm grip on her hips, he pulled her up until her knees rested on the seat on either side of his legs. Meanwhile her head lay on the floor of the limo and she let out a girlish giggle. His fingers played along her buttocks, under her thong and into the crevice in which it disappeared. He pulled the thin strip of fabric out of the crevice and licked the length of the tender pink skin that hungered for him.

He worked his tongue over the flesh, titillating and thrilling, teasing her mercilessly one moment, then lavishing her with such exquisite pleasure, she was certain all of New York could hear her feral cries.

Just as her orgasm swept over her, Errol reached down and took a hold of her waist and pulled her up into a sitting position. Wasting little time, he sat her on his shaft and proceeded to pump her with surprising speed and ardor.

Taryn took on the pumping motion, freeing Errol's hand so that he could take a firm hold of the bouncing orbs. He filled her, enthralled her, and completed her. Once again she found herself drowning in too many emotions. The sex was irresistibly great, but she couldn't keep her heart from becoming involved.

Damn, she thought as she sat back on Errol's lap. *Bobby's right. I can't just let it be sex. I can't keep from falling in love with him.*

Chapter 13

Fully dressed and sitting properly in their respective seats, Errol and Taryn enjoyed the tour around the city.

"There's an interesting exhibit at the Met. Do you like art?"

She hesitated. "Not that I don't admire artists and their talent, but I guess I just never had the time to really appreciate it."

"Maybe we can take the time someday to get you caught up."

The limo turned into Central Park and Errol flicked a switch to lower the window that separated them from Russell. "Can you pull over? We'll go for a little walk."

The car rolled to a stop and Errol popped out before Russell could come around. "We'll roam around for twenty minutes or so and be right back."

"Take your time, sir."

Hand in hand they strolled down a meandering path. "I can't resist a stroll in the park, especially in the fall. It smells great, and the color of the leaves makes it absolutely gorgeous. Besides, you can't beat this weather. It's the perfect ending to any day."

"Funny. I can't really imagine you strolling through the park."

"Okay, so it's not something I do every day, but it is something I enjoy. It was one of my favorite places when I was a kid, and I still love it. How 'bout you?"

"I can't say I really have any connection with Central Park. I think we might have driven through it once when I was a kid, but it was quick and that was it."

"How can you have lived in New York all your life without picnicking in Central Park or taking a carriage ride, or skipping stones in the pond?"

Taryn shrugged. "My mother has always been... how can I say...?" She almost choked and chuckled on the description that came to mind. "Pragmatic. She had to be. When she wasn't working at the restaurant, she was helping us with homework, keeping a clean house, cooking and everything else that comes along with raising two kids all by herself." She stopped suddenly and turned to Errol.

"Don't get me wrong. My mother has always been great with us. Amidst all that, she had time to play Monopoly with us at least once a week and when we were really little she'd take us to the local park every once in a while."

"Do you think you missed out on being a kid because your dad skipped out?"

"No, not really. I just had a childhood that was a little different from some kids... then again, I think there are a lot of kids out there who've probably gone through similar stuff... or worse."

"What doesn't kill you makes you stronger, huh?"

"I guess. You know, a lot of my friends had it easy. Both parents worked, money came in, they never had to work... I can't say I didn't envy them. Just before graduating from high school, I started to wonder if I'd be able to make it. I was going to school all week, working three nights a week plus weekends, taking care of Bobby in whatever capacity I could and I was trying to come up with great recipes to impress every culinary school I knew."

"I'm sure this made you the capable and industrious girl you are today."

"Yeah, I can't deny it was a great training ground. Bobby was a young teenager and part of him wanted to rebel and raise hell, but he's always had this part of him that wanted to be the man about the house. You know, protective and everything."

"So, I noticed."

They stopped to let a horse drawn carriage pass. Taryn looked at the large white horse with adoration then glanced at the couple in the carriage and smiled. Holding hands, they cuddled close together and gazed out at the gorgeous colors of the park. For a second, Taryn felt a tinged of jealousy. The couple was so much in love. The woman had no doubt the man she was with, loved her. Taryn swallowed. She had passion; she had excitement with Errol, but did she have his undying love? Was she the one for him or the one of many?

"I have an idea," Errol said as he put his arm around her shoulders. "I think we both need a day off."

"That we need one is one thing; that we can have one is another."

"Let me take care of it. Tomorrow I'll have an expert team at Sam's. I'll contact everyone tonight, give specific instructions and tomorrow, you and I are going to go to Coney Island."

"That's impossible, Errol."

"Let me take care of it," Errol took her hand and kissed each knuckle. "I want a day with you just enjoying yourself, outside of the restaurant. Please. If not for you, for me."

"Why?" Taryn asked, looking into his brilliant blue eyes.

Errol licked his lips. "It's adorable that you still don't realize how you've captivated me, Taryn.

***

With a fluffy cloud of pink cotton candy in one hand and a caramel apple in the other, Taryn enjoyed her sugar rush as they waited in line for a ride on the roller coaster.

"That is so high," she whispered as she looked up and up. "I can't believe I'm going to go up that high?"

"Afraid of heights?" He plucked off a wad of cotton candy and set it on his tongue.

"I don't know. We'll find out soon." Thrilled and a little intimidated, she watched the screaming and excited kids who rode the roller coaster to unbelievable heights. "Maybe eating all this isn't the best idea."

Errol followed her gaze. "It doesn't look that bad."

She shot him an amused gaze. He was being so unerringly sweet.

Since arriving, Taryn noticed how girls were drawn to Errol. They turned to look at him, licked their lips provocatively and tried to give him the eye. She'd even seen a few bolder girls come up to him and try to engage him in a conversation, all while completely ignoring her presence.

Through it all, Errol was polite, but showed a distinct lack of interest in any of them, even the buxom blonde who was all too proud to come shove her newly inflated chest up to his. He dedicated his full attention to Taryn. Every chance he got, he wrapped his arms around her, held her hand and kissed her.

Errol leaned over her to take a bite of the caramel apple Taryn was eating before she threw the core and stick away just as they arrived to the head of the line.

"Front, middle or back?" Errol said.

Without answering, Taryn headed to a middle stall, but a serious case of the jitters took over.

"You okay?"

"Yep." Her gaze darted over the faces of the returning passengers. All were thrilled, smiling, laughing and many were eager to do it all over again. "Yep, I'm fine."

"Having second thoughts?"

"No. I want to do this."

"This may sound like a silly question, but, have you ever been on a roller coaster… I mean, any roller coaster?"

A little put off by his question, she turned to him. "Of course I have." Biting her lip she looked down at the empty seat and hesitated. "Of course it was the kiddy roller coaster at one of those fly by night carnivals they set up at the mall."

"If it makes you feel any better, I've never been on one of these things either. We can be roller coaster virgins together." He took her hand and pressed it reassuringly.

Taryn got into the little red car and allowed the young employee to secure her in. She glanced at Errol.

"Ready?" he said with a wink.

She reached for his hand as the series of cars began to chugalug their way up, and up, and up. The view was incredible, beautiful, and breathtaking until the moment they reached the summit and quickly plummeted into the steel belly of the beast. Her screams, at first frightened and horrified, nearly drowned out the roar of the beast as it twirled them around, and around, up and down in a tailspin, in a corkscrew in a ridiculous barrel roll.

As the wind whipped her hair back and the spinning motions tickled her, her screams quickly filled with glee and the excitement of the next ride. By the time the car came to a stop, she radiated joy.

"Okay, we have to do that again."

They went on to ride the roller coaster three more times, then moved on to a calming ride on the carousel and finally a quiet and romantic stroll on the beach.

"In sixth grade, the whole class was brought here," Taryn confided. "That is, the students who were able to pay the fee and get their parents' permission."

"You didn't get to go?"

She pressed her lips together and shook her head. "I remember telling my mom that I didn't really want to go anyway. I mean, I knew she couldn't afford it. I didn't want her to feel guilty about my missing out on that trip. She worked so hard at the restaurant and, no matter how many hours she put in, it seemed there was never enough money for extras." Taryn stopped talking as a wave of dark frightening memories filled her mind. It wasn't always so hard for her mother. Taryn remembered seeing her mother always dressed up when her father was around. It was different when he was there. They had money for things back then. If she wanted, and her father was around, she would have gone to Coney Island all the time.

"But you would have liked to go?" Errol asked, shaking Taryn out of her thoughts.

"Hmm...yes. When Mrs. Wellington, my teacher, surprised us with the announcement that we were all going to Coney Island, I was ecstatic. It seemed everyone I knew had gone at least once in their lifetime and I had only heard about it. But the moment she mentioned how much it would cost, I knew I wouldn't be able to go. The following Monday when the kids all came back to school, they exchanged stories, remembering the rides they'd liked the most and all the junk they'd eaten and how much fun they'd had. I tried to shrug it off, but it really killed me. I was dying of envy, but I just listened to them and smiled like an idiot."

He draped his arm over her shoulder and pulled her close. "I know I can't make up for the things you missed in your childhood, and I want to, but..."

"This has been great, Errol. I might not be twelve, but, I have to admit, a few times today, I felt like I was. It was perfect, from the cotton candy in my hair, to the caramel in my teeth to the turning in my stomach." She stopped and spun around to face him. "Besides, I got to do it all with you. That's a lot cooler than doing it all with a bunch of pimply faced kids, right?"

Errol kissed her hungrily for several seconds and pulled her so close to him, she can feel the hardness of him tight against her soft skin. "It's certainly a lot sexier." He pulled away enough to gently cup her face. "Whatever you missed out on when you were a child, I want to fulfill."

Taryn gulped at the intensity in his blue eyes as he stared at her, his thumbs rubbing her lower lip. Did he really mean it?

"Why?" Taryn asked.

"Because," Errol said so softly it was like a whisper against her cheek, "I want to see your eyes smile like it did today. I want to see your face light up with wonder as you experience things like riding a roller coaster for the first time."

"You love that I'm so inexperienced in the world then," Taryn said.

"No," Errol took her hand. "If I wanted someone naïve, I can take my pick of anyone, but no, I wanted you from the first time I saw your photo and read about your desires in life. Something about you intrigued me from the start."

"That could be creepy," Taryn smiled.

"Or," Errol said, leaning in, "it could be because you're not prepared for the passion I could unleash in you."

His fingers played with her neck and collarbone, sending thrills of excitement through Taryn. The day had been a perfectly sweet day, but she knew, just looking at Errol that her night with him tonight would be nothing sweet.

"In case you didn't know," Errol whispered against her ear, "I enjoyed this day with you immensely. Now, my sweet Taryn, I can't wait to begin this evening with you."

Chapter 14

"Hey," Errol said as he came into Sam's kitchen and wrapped his arms around Taryn's waist from behind, pulling her in for a kiss. "With things quieting down here, how 'bout coming over to La Benicoise? You haven't even come to see it yet."

"I haven't had time, Errol."

"You have time now. The crew can handle the few remaining customers out there. Not to brag, but La Benicoise has customers coming in for dinner well past midnight. You'll get a chance to see…"

"What… how a real restaurant is run?"

"That's not what I was going to say."

"Maybe, but I'm sure it's not too far off."

"It's different, that's all. Throw off that apron, and come on."

Minutes later they were entering the culinary palace Errol had created. The dining room was large, but managed to feel intimate. The décor was somber and refined, but comfortable; the kind of place patrons wanted to stay and linger over every aspect of their meal.

"This is impressive." Taryn ran her hand over the back of a plush, stuffed chair. The stemware on the table glistened and the silver gleamed over a pristine white linen napkin set atop a crisp black tablecloth.

Several couples sat enjoying a quiet meal, while many groups of four, six and even eight held animated conversations over an expensive glass of wine and a sumptuous late night dinner.

"Come to the kitchen to see how we put it all together."

The words she'd spoken earlier reverberated in her head; how a real restaurant is run. Large, well lit and expensively equipped, the kitchen easily allowed a dozen employees to work at their stations with ample room. The flow of dishes being prepared and brought out to customers was fluid and seamless.

"Okay," she said. "Now I'm really impressed. I mean, I knew large restaurants had to be well run, but I've never seen anything like this."

"I have to admit that I'm well surrounded. I handpicked every employee you see here, right down to the busboys. I read and re-read each of their résumés, I checked out all their references and I personally interviewed them and put them to the test."

"That must have been quite a task."

"It took weeks, but it was well worth it. Look at how they all work together; like one."

A waitress noticed Errol and came up to him. "I'm sorry to bother you, Mr. King, but a patron saw you come in and would like to personally congratulate you."

"Thank you, Natalie. I'll be right out." He turned to Taryn. "I'll leave you to admire my team for a moment."

Taryn grinned and waved him away.

With every order that came in, commands for various portions of every dish were call out, executed, plated and brought out to the waiting customers. Impressed and a little envious, Taryn watched the quick pace of the employees until she noticed Suzanne eyeing her from the far corner of the kitchen.

Though she wore the same white jacket as all the other employees in the kitchen, her voluptuous sensuality was in no way diminished. She sashayed her way to Taryn, her eyes dark and menacing above the deceitful smile.

"Taryn, is it not?"

"Yes," Taryn said as she controlled every part of her body that fought to fidget. "Nice to see you again."

"And what brings you out of the slums and into a real restaurant like La Benicoise?" Her tone, in complete contrast to her words, was polite and amiable.

Instead of responding to the venom of Suzanne's words, Taryn opted to play nice. "I know I still have a lot to learn when it comes to running a restaurant. I've never seen a kitchen run like this. It's spectacular."

"Indeed." Suzanne shot Taryn a disgusted up and down gaze. "I assume it was Errol's idea."

"Yes, he did bring me here. He went out to see a patron."

A chuckle rumbled ominously in Suzanne's chest. "You're a cute, perky little thing and I'm surprised Errol still finds something in you that interests him, but, rest assured, my young Taryn, your time is almost up. "

Taryn hesitated as she sought her best response. Get angry and spit at the bitch? Play sweet and just bat her lashes innocently? Accuse her of being jealous? She clasped her hands together in front of her and simply nodded.

"I've known Errol for a long time." She unbuttoned her jacket and pulled the flaps back as she set her hands firmly on her hips, exposing the skin tight, hot red cocktail dress underneath. "A very long time."

Taryn swallowed the huge ball of discomfort that lodged in her throat and kept her mute.

"You have nothing on me, sweetie. You're just a plaything to occupy his time while I'm busy here. I admit it. I got ambitious when we started this restaurant and I concentrated all my attention into turning La Benicoise into the success it's become. Now that everything is running smoothly, I have plenty of energy to put elsewhere, and I'm hungry for Errol. I'm hungry for the sweaty and sleepless nights he and I used to share. I'm sure he had fun with you, but he's also made it clear that he's eager to resume our relationship."

Taryn's eyes widened in horror for a flash before she clenched her teeth and glanced at the doorway Errol had disappeared through.

"Oh, did Errol forget to tell you about our relationship?"

"Actually, I think he might have just forgotten all about your relationship altogether." The moment the words were out, Taryn regretted the snide comment; not because they were mean spirited, but because she knew Suzanne would have a strong retort.

Tilting her head back, Suzanne let out a raunchy laugh and reached out to caress Taryn's cheek. "Ah, you wish, my dear. You wish." She turned on her heel and returned to work.

By the time Errol returned, it was as if nothing had happened, except for the fuming rage that bellowed deep within Taryn. She smiled at Errol, but felt the tension on her lips, on her face and in her clenched fists.

"Benoit Radisson," Errol said. "He's an acquaintance from Paris. I must have told him a dozen times to drop by if he was ever in New York, so…"

"That's nice of him." Taryn heard the hard cool tone that came out of her mouth, but Errol missed it.

"Come on. We'll go tell Suzanne we're here." He put his hand to her elbow and when Taryn resisted, he turned to her. "You okay?"

"Actually, no. I'm a bit tired. I think it's time I went home."

He chuckled. "Don't be silly. You're not tired. It's just the impression you have from watching this whirlwind. It's enough to exhaust anyone." He tugged on her arm.

"Errol, I really don't feel like it."

"But Suzanne can give you such insight. If you were to just watch her for..."

No longer able to contain her anger, Taryn yanked her arm free and stepped back. "I said, no."

"What's gotten into you? A minute ago you were enchanted and now you look like you're disgusted."

"All right. If you must know, Suzanne and I exchanged a few words. And, you know what? You're right, she did give me insight, but not into the way you run your restaurant, Errol, but rather the way you run your sex life."

Errol clenched his jaw as his eyes darkened.

"Yeah," Taryn droned. "That's right. She told me about the two of you, and she seemed quite happy to do so."

He reached out for her. "Taryn..."

"Don't," she ordered as she stepped back. "Don't touch me just now, Errol."

"What do you want me to tell you?"

"The truth, maybe."

"Okay, but this isn't the place or time."

Taryn gazed past Errol and saw Suzanne, a cocky grin on her face as she glanced their way while taking care of every order that came in.

Stepping back just a few paces, Taryn found an out of the way corner and stared Errol down. "This is as good a place as any, and I seriously doubt you'll have another time to explain all this."

"Taryn, I did have a life before I met you."

"I know that."

"Okay, so, yes, Suzanne and I…" He clenched his jaw and shifted his weight from one leg to the other. "We had a relationship that was more than professional."

"You went to bed with her."

"It was a long time ago."

"You went to bed with her."

"Taryn…"

"You went to bed with her."

"Yes. Yes. What more do you want me to tell you? Taryn, I met her, we worked together and the relationship turned personal, but it was all a long time ago and there's nothing…"

"Don't you dare try to tell there's nothing going on between you two. She made it perfectly clear that she wants you and she said you've been hinting about resuming your relationship with her."

"She's fantasizing aloud, Taryn. I have no intention of doing anything with her other than running this restaurant. We don't even sit to have a casual cup of coffee together."

"And why should I believe you?"

"Taryn, even if I weren't involved with you, I would not want to start up with her again. It's over. We got together, had a little bit of fun, and now I've moved on."

"So you can do the same with me? Have a little bit of fun and move on?"

"No."

"Why not?"

"This isn't the same. We're not the same. My relationship with you isn't..."

"Yeah, right, I get it. I'm the cute and perky little girl you can sexually enlighten while she's the experienced vixen who... well, I don't really want to have to think about what she did to and for you."

"You're making a big deal out of something that was over before I even met you, Taryn."

"Okay then, if it's really over, if you have nothing going on with this woman, if you have no intention of starting a new romance with this woman, then fire her."

He brought his hand to his chest as if she'd struck him. "Taryn," he said as he chuckled uncomfortably. "I can't do that."

"Why not?"

"I have this business. I have the restaurant to run. Professionally speaking, I need her."

"I'm sure there are a hundred well-qualified sous-chefs out there who would love to work for you."

"You'd be surprised. Finding someone as qualified, competent and dedicated as Suzanne isn't that easy."

"You mean finding someone who'll fuck you the way she does isn't that easy." Taryn stormed out of the kitchen and stomped through the dining room.

"Taryn," Errol called after her.

Chapter 15

Taryn lost count of the number of times Errol called, the number of times she saw his number and ignored it. She lost count of the endless apologetic texts and the messages he left at Sam's.

"I'm going to go home and check in on Mom," Taryn said to Bobby as she ignored another text and pulled off her apron. "I need to get some air." Bobby was right, Errol was the kind of man who would break her heart. He was an experienced sex god, player, man whore, Cassanova; while Taryn was Miss First Timer.

"What should I do if Errol drops by again?"

"The same thing you've been telling him; that I don't want him here."

He leaned against the doorjamb and looked at her. "You know, I'm the first to think you should be careful when it comes to guys like him, but…"

"Please don't tell me you're going to take his defense, Bobby." She put the lunch she'd prepared for her mother in a paper bag.

"No, I'm not going to defend him, but I just think you're being a little hard on the guy. I mean, it's normal that he has a past."

"I know that, Bobby." Taryn reached for her jacket and shrugged it on. "I have no objections to that. I object to the fact that his past is right there in his present."

"Do you really think that's fair?"

She looked at him in disbelief. "I can't believe it. You're taking his side. You've been on my back since day one about being careful not to get too attached, not to fall in love, not to trust him and now…"

"I never said you shouldn't trust him, I just said to keep your eyes open."

"Well," she said as she patted her brother's cheek. "That's what I'm doing, little brother. I'm keeping my eyes wide open." She turned to open the door. "I'll be back in an hour."

As she drove home, Taryn turned the radio on and tuned it to her favorite station. She needed an upbeat song to make her forget Errol and put aside her argument with

Bobby. More than anything, she wanted to keep this recent development with Errol from her mother. She needed a good song to lift her into a good mood.

"Hey, Mom," she called out as she opened the apartment door. "I brought you something for lunch."

"You're just in time," Samantha called from her room. "I'm famished."

Taryn tossed her jacket on the sofa and went into her mother's bedroom. "Sorry, I couldn't get here earlier."

"Hey, I'm thrilled. If you're here late it's because things are rocking and rolling at the restaurant, right?"

"Right, Mom." Taryn pulled her prepared lunch out of the bag for her Mom. "Today, we have a nice shell pasta with a delicate garlic sauce and shrimp."

"Sure smells good."

"It should still be hot." Taryn helped her mom sit up and pulled a chair up to the bed for herself. "How'd your therapy go this morning?"

Sam tasted the pasta. "This is great. Perfect." She dug in for more and spoke as she ate. "Yolanda has been putting me through the wringer. It's unavoidable. I finish my therapy and I'm bitching and complaining like you wouldn't believe."

"Well, I'm sure she's just doing what's best for you."

"I know. I just wish it could be a little easier."

"It'll get easier. And soon you'll be back at Sam's. Everyone really misses you, Mom."

"Yolanda thinks I might be strong enough to go out for a visit... maybe next week."

"I won't say anything to anyone. That way everyone will be surprised to see you."

"Good, cause it will probably be a spot check while I'm at it."

"You won't be disappointed. Things are running pretty smooth. Our new employees, Kyle and Lauren, are really fast learners, and I told you how Arnie is really coming up to the plate."

"Gee, if things keep going so well, I might just be able to retire."

"Yeah, right. You... retire. And what would you do with all your free time."

Samantha set her lunch aside and reached for Taryn's hand. "What's going on, sweetie?"

"Well, like I just said, things are..."

"No, not the restaurant... you."

"With the new employees, I have a bit more time, and…"

"Taryn," Samantha said as she squeezed her hand. "I didn't want to say anything. I wanted to give you time to figure out whatever it is you need to figure out, but something has changed. You've changed this past week. You come in here smiling and you're putting on a brave face, but you can't hide the sadness in your eyes. What's going on?"

Tears lined her lashes and she dropped her gaze to the comforter on the bed. "Please don't say you told me so."

Samantha remained silent a long moment. "This is about your relationship with that interesting person you've avoided talking to me about?"

"I'm sorry. It's not that I didn't want to confide in you, but with everything that's going on."

"Okay, I'll buy that… for now, but what did he do to leave you so heartbroken?"

Taryn looked pointedly at her mother. "He works with this ungodly sexy woman, a woman who has the hots for him."

"That's hardly his fault, dear."

"They once had an intimate relationship."

"Oh, okay. I can understand how that can upset you, but, is it over?"

"He says it is."

"And?"

"And she says it's not." Taryn grimaced as she thought of her conversation with Suzanne. "You should see the way she looks at him, Mom. You should see the way she looks at me. My God, you should see the way she looks."

"Perhaps you should consider how this man is looking at you."

"Damn it, Mom, not you, too."

"What do you mean?"

"Bobby was taking his side this morning, saying I was being too hard on him, and now you. I asked him to fire her, Mom and he refused. He's working with a hot and sexy woman who's made it clear she wants him and he refuses to take into consideration how I feel in all this."

"And how do you feel?"

"I hate it. I hate it that he's there every day, every night working side by side with her."

"Why?"

"What do you mean, why? Because, Mom. Because I don't want him going to bed with her. Because I want him to be with me."

"Because you feel insecure?"

Taryn shrugged. "I guess."

"Do you love him?"

Pulling her hand free of her mom's, she sat back and sighed. "Oh, hell, I don't know. Sometimes I think I might, then I think I shouldn't, then I realize I do despite everything."

"It's not easy, is it?"

"Damn, no." She crossed her arms over her chest. "This sucks."

Samantha let out a hearty laugh. "It can, at times, but, honey, I don't want you to turn into an old, cynical, prune like me. I admit I was a little bitter when everything went down with your father and the reason I left him, but you can't allow yourself to drown in that bitterness. When's the last time you spoke to…"

"Errol. His name is Errol. Last week when he told me everything."

"I don't want to tell you what to do, but I'd just suggest you keep an open mind."

Taryn checked her watch. "Maybe in a few more days, when I've simmered off a bit, I'll consider keeping an open mind, but for now…" She shook her head. "I'm just too disgusted by the whole thing to even think about talking to him."

"You know best what's good for you."

With a heavy heart, Taryn got up and put the chair back in its corner and returned to kiss her mother on the cheek. "Is there anything you need before I leave?"

"Everything's good, honey."

"Okay, see you later." As Taryn walked out, she realized just how much she'd needed to talk to her mother about Errol. The simple act of spilling everything cleared her head somewhat, though she still had some way to go.

She got in her car, put the radio up loud and took to the streets. Pounding out the beat of a sassy song on her steering wheel, Taryn maneuvered her car through the streets and only realized once she'd crossed the bridge that she was heading into Manhattan, heading in the direction of La Benicoise instead of to Sam's.

"Damn it," she cursed as she turned the car around.

"It's a beautiful day here in New York City," the radio announcer said. "But I must caution people who are thinking of driving through the Upper East Side. We have a fire raging and we're told traffic is being diverted…"

The Upper East Side, Taryn thought with horror. That's where Errol's restaurant is.

"For now we don't have too many details to give you, except that the fire is being brought under control as we speak. We had an earlier report that stated the newly opened restaurant, La Benicoise, might be at the heart of the flames, but that hasn't been confirmed yet."

Time stopped. Staring blindly in front of her, Taryn pressed on the brakes while car horns blared at her. People yelled at her, but it was only when an angry driver got out of his car and came to knock on her window that she shook off her daze and drove off.

She turned her radio to a news station.

"Fire trucks line the streets and many of the buildings surrounding La Benicoise have been evacuated. So far we've had no word of injuries aside from a few cases of smoke inhalation, although we did hear of a brave citizen who entered the flaming building in order to save an employee. The employee and brave citizen are said to be doing fine. If you look out your window, there's a good chance you'll see the plume of smoke rising into this clear afternoon sky."

Taryn had spotted the cloud of smoke just seconds earlier. No one was hurt, she thought, at least, as far as they knew. As she got closer and closer to the restaurant, traffic slowed down and soon stopped. Ignoring the fact that she'd get a hefty parking ticket, she pulled over and abandoned the car to walk the rest of the way.

At the barricade a police officer stopped her.

"Please, my boyf..." Her heart raced. "I know someone. I have to find him."

From a distance, Taryn spotted Errol, his face black with smoke, his clothes tattered and torn. "Please, he's right there. Please just let me go see him."

"I'm sorry, Miss, but I can't let anyone through just yet. The firefighters say it's under control, and they should be giving the green light any minute now."

For an endless and tortured six minutes, Taryn stood at the perimeter of the scene, helpless and anxious.

Errol brought his blackened hands to his face as he looked at the devastation. Even from a distance, Taryn could see how distraught he was and she longed to put her arms around him and console him.

A trio of firefighters, headed by Matt, came up to him. Errol shook their hands and patted their shoulders as he forced an appreciative smile.

"All's clear, Miss," the police officer said as he pulled back the barricade.

Elated, she thanked him and headed toward Errol. She could hear his words of gratitude as well as Matt's words of encouragement. All was not lost. The kitchen was all but destroyed, but the dining room was salvageable.

"Well, it's all thanks to you guys," Errol said. "I owe you one, big time."

"All in a day's work, sir."

"Well, as soon as my doors open again, I want to have you all here as my guests."

"That's very generous," Matt said. "But that won't be necessary."

"I insist."

Just as Taryn came up behind Errol, she gagged as Suzanne came up to him. A whole panel of her skirt was torn loose, exposing her thigh right up to her bright red thong. She'd also lost several buttons of her chef's jacket leaving the front open for all to see her generous bosom under the flimsy camisole she wore.

"Oh, Errol, it's just awful. I still can't believe..." She threw herself into his arms. "I just can't believe it."

Errol put his arm around her waist. "I know. It's awful, but at least no one got hurt. The insurance will cover the damages and we should be up and running in no time."

"I can't believe your optimism at a time like this. You're incredible, Errol." She looked at him with open admiration. "Oh, before I forget, a fire inspector or something like that was looking for you. He wanted to ask you a few questions. Come, I'll introduce you."

Matt looked up and noticed Taryn, bringing Errol to follow his gaze to her. His eyes widened in surprise, but Suzanne refused to let go of him. "Taryn, I'm so happy you came."

"Come on, Errol. The inspector is waiting for you."

"Don't go away," Errol pleaded. "I'll be right back."

Taryn offered him a slight and non-committal nod. She ignored the relief she heard in his voice and concentrated solely on the woman who so brazenly draped herself over him. Overwhelmed by too many conflicting emotions, she turned her attention to Matt the moment Errol walked away.

"I'm happy to see you're okay, Matt. I hear this was quite a fire."

"It got a little hairy there for a minute. The fire threatened to sneak its way over to the neighboring buildings. As you can see now, the worse is over. How d'you find out about the fire?"

"The radio. Actually they were telling everyone to avoid coming to the area... you know, traffic and all."

"But since this is your friend's restaurant..."

She shrugged and her gaze wandered to Errol who stood only yards away talking to an inspector. Suzanne never let go of him and she kept her breasts pressed tightly against his arm. Disgusted, Taryn brought her gaze back to Matt. "Having my own restaurant I can understand how heartbreaking it is to see something you've worked so hard to build go up in smoke."

"It's really not as bad as it looks. A good clean up and the replacement of a few pieces of equipment and he should be opening his doors again soon."

"Good. That's good to hear." She shoved her hands in her pockets and shifted. "It's been a while since I've seen you. How've you been?"

"Not bad. Busy."

"I haven't seen you at Sam's lately. Were you served a bad plate?" She grinned and tried to shake off the dismal sense of failure brought on by the ongoing sexual onslaught of Suzanne on Errol.

"Of course not." He met her gaze, unsure of her question. "I got the sense I was hanging around too much."

"That's ridiculous, Matt."

"Not only that, but I transferred to another firehouse. Going to Sam's is a little more out of the way than before."

"Oh, well, that's legitimate. Also explains what you're doing all the way out here. You know, we never did get the chance to just go out one quiet evening."

Still unsure, he offered her a reserved smile.

"It doesn't have to be a big, romantic production or anything, but I think it'd be nice to just sit down together and talk without any distractions."

"Sounds good. How 'bout this Saturday?"

She cringed. "Saturday is about the worst day for me. Monday would be perfect."

"Great."

Chapter 16

Called away by a superior, Matt left Taryn to watch the scene alone. Not knowing whether she should stay or go, she paced, stepping forward and backward, then from side to side and finally around in a semi-circle.

In the distance, she caught an occasional glimpse of Errol with Suzanne. Though it hurt to see him with the sexy siren, Taryn found her gaze repeatedly seeking the pair out.

Her heart wanted desperately to see a clear sign that he wasn't interested in the woman who so blatantly threw herself at him, but in her mind, she realized she knew Errol too well to really expect anything of the sort.

He was a womanizer, the kind of man who loved women, but could never love *a* woman. His eyes wandered, and constantly sought a new challenge, a new conquest, and a new plaything to occupy his time.

"But, he's already had Suzanne," Taryn muttered to herself. "She should be old news by now."

As curiosity got the better of her, she found herself inching closer and closer to the conversation Errol was having with the inspector.

"We'll try to find the source of the fire as soon as possible," the inspector said. "I know you must be eager to get everything running again."

"It's not a question of being eager," Suzanne said with a hint of haughty impatience. "We have obligations." She turned to Errol. "We have a least three major reservations at the restaurant in the next week alone. Important reservations for important people."

"We'll never be ready by next week," Errol said. "We'll have a few phone calls to make."

Taryn stood within earshot, but was careful not to intrude on the conversation. The inspector noticed her, but paid no attention to her, but Suzanne spotted her and her gaze immediately darkened.

Intimidated and weighed down by an increasingly heavy sense of defeat, Taryn took a step back, but Errol turned to look her way and his eyes lit up.

"Taryn!" He turned back to the inspector. "Just a second." Stepping up to Taryn, he reached out to touch her arm. "This is taking a little longer than I expected. They seem to have reason to believe the fire might have been deliberately set."

"I'm sorry to hear that."

"Look, I just have to discuss a few things, but then I'm free. I want to see you, Taryn. I want to see you tonight."

"Um..."

"I'm so happy you stopped by. It means a lot to me."

"Errol," Suzanne called, her voice almost shrill with irritation. "We have to finish up here. I'm going to have a lot of work to do once we get through this."

Without turning back to look at Suzanne, Errol squeezed Taryn's arm. "I know you probably have to rush back to Sam's soon, but if you could stick around a bit longer... I really want to see you..."

Taryn nodded, but was unable to find her voice to say a word.

Regret shadowed his eyes as he pressed his lips together, nodded and turned away.

Walking away with his words ringing in her ears, Taryn allowed her heart to wonder. He spoke so softly, so sincerely, so sweetly... it had to mean something. Maybe he'd told her the truth about Suzanne. After all, she knew he had a past.

"Hey," Matt called as he made his way back to her. "Sorry I had to leave you like that."

"No problem." She turned and shot a glance at Errol as he walked toward the smoking rubble with the fire inspector and Suzanne.

"You know, I was thinking... about our date. I know the perfect place to have a nice, quiet and secluded night under the stars."

In a deft little step that left Matt frowning in confusion, Taryn spun around, allowing her to face Matt, all while keeping a distant eye on Errol. "Sounds perfect, Matt." Though she heard him and told herself to tear her eyes off Errol and Suzanne and concentrate on him, she couldn't. Suzanne stayed close to Errol and her gaze sizzled as she looked up into his eyes.

From where she stood, Taryn couldn't see Errol's reaction, but she could easily imagine it; the provocative grin, the wicked gleam in his eye, the hungry swipe of his tongue over his lips. She could even imagine the reflection of Suzanne's breast reflected in Errol's eyes.

With tortured intensity, she imagined them together, naked, sweaty and in impossible positions. What tricks had Suzanne used to keep Errol interested? What tricks did she have planned to get him back?

All the love she'd seen in his eyes just moments earlier faded as she observed Suzanne put a possessive arm around Errol's shoulders. Like an illusion, a trick of the eye... an experienced playboy stringing his little puppet along.

Taryn turned brazen eyes to Matt and slipped her arm through his. "You know, I'm really looking forward to this date you have planned. I think a night under the stars will be great."

As they slowly strolled away from the laid out fire hoses and past the barricade, Taryn leaned into him, held onto him and smiled invitingly at him... until she reached the spot where she'd left her car.

"Damn it. No. This can't be."

"What's wrong?"

"My car. I left it right here. Oh, damn. Of all things."

"Look, don't worry about it. I think I know where they brought it."

Shaking her head, Taryn looked at the empty parking space. "Yeah, but getting a cab out here with all this mess is going to be near impossible."

"How 'bout a quick ride on a fire truck?"

With a gleeful smile smacked on her face, she turned to him. "Really?"

"Sure. You're in a bind... I'm sure no one will mind. You can come back to the firehouse, and from there I'll bring you to your car."

"You're a sweetheart."

***

Leaning against a locker upstairs in the firehouse, Taryn watched Matt change into his street clothes. She couldn't help but notice the smooth skin stretched across the bulging muscles of his chest, shoulders and arms. How many women had fantasized being swept out of a burning building by such a strong and capable fire fighter as Matt?

And here she was, with him all to herself.

"How'd you like the ride?" He looked up and grinned when he caught her peeping gaze.

Taryn patted her heated cheeks. "My face hurts from smiling so much."

As he pulled a tight t-shirt over his head, she was tempted to reach out and run her fingers along his chest. Her anger at Errol and the heartache he'd caused left her eager to find new emotions with a new man.

It was time she put Errol behind her, and Matt was the perfect guy to do just that.

Slipping into his sneakers, he looked up at her. "Ready to go?"

"Lead the way."

In his car, Matt was silent for a long while. "You know, I'm really glad I bumped into you today," he finally said.

"Me, too." Beaming, she touched his arm to emphasize her words. "The timing couldn't be more perfect."

"Hey, I know you have to hurry back to the restaurant, but do you think we could stop by Joe's Pizza... for old time's sake? And I am really starving."

"Oh, my God. I'd forgotten all about that place," she said with an amused giggle.

"It might not necessarily be the fancy kind of food you're used to, but..."

"Are you kidding? It has the best New York style pizza. That sounds great, Matt." She pulled her cell phone out of her purse. "Bobby, hey I need to ask you a favor. I'm..." She checked her watch and realized just how late she was. She'd missed the entire lunch rush.

"Yeah, I heard about the fire at Benicoise," Bobby said.

"Oh."

"That's really too bad. Errol must really be bummed out. Don't worry about coming back right away. I understand if you want to spend a bit of time with him."

A little flustered, Taryn didn't correct him. "Thanks for understanding, Bobby. I won't come in too late."

"That was easy enough," Matt said.

"He owes me one. In fact, he owes me several."

Matt pulled up across the street from their favorite teenage haunt. Nestled between a barbershop and a dry cleaner, the tiny pizzeria had always had a cozy and friendly atmosphere.

"Wow," Taryn whispered as she reluctantly got out of the car. "I didn't remember this part of the neighborhood being this bad. Wasn't there a park over there?"

"Yeah. Turned out more kids were going there to deal drugs than go down the slide, you know what I mean." He offered his arm as they crossed the deserted street and opened the restaurant door for her. "Funny how things can change so fast."

"Yeah."

Inside, the restaurant was quiet except for a table of four older men who sat chatting in Italian.

Matt ordered, and when the waiter brought the pizza to the table, Taryn was flooded with a ton of memories, all of them wafting on the spicy aromas of tomato and cheese.

"Remember when everyone had turned their backs on Cathy? We'd all come here without telling her. We were so mean."

He nodded. "All because she'd supposedly kissed Elaine's boyfriend."

"I can't believe how silly we were back then."

"Don't worry. Five years from now you'll probably think that you were pretty silly now. My uncle once told me that phenomenon never ends. Even when you're sixty, you look back and think how naïve and juvenile you were when you were a mere lad of fifty."

Taryn laughed as she chomped on the pizza crust. It was so easy being with him, so effortless. She looked at him, the image of his muscular nude torso still so clear in his mind.

- 201 -

"Are we still good for Monday?"

"Sure. Why not?"

They ate their pizza while reminiscing about the fun and mischief they'd had only a few short years earlier. By the time they headed out, Taryn felt nostalgic. At his car, Matt came around to unlock the door for Taryn, but two young men came up to them.

"Nice night to be out, isn't it?" the tall, clean cut guy said.

Instantly, the hair at the nape of her neck stood on end.

"Yeah," the scruffy, long haired one said. "We were wondering if you could give us a hand."

"We're late enough as it is, fellas," Matt said. He opened the door for Taryn, but the tall young man kicked it shut.

"That's no way to treat someone who's asking for a favor."

"What do you guys want?"

"Well, your wallet would be a nice start."

"Look, guys I just want…"

"This isn't Let's Make a Deal, buddy. Hand over your wallet and, if it looks interesting enough, we'll let it go at that." His menacing gaze dropped to Taryn's purse.

Matt reached out to put a protective arm in front of Taryn. Stepping in front of her, he looked at the two would-be muggers straight on. "I've got fifteen bucks in my pockets and a maxed out credit card in my wallet. Sorry, but I've got nothing that could interest you."

"Then we'll have to ask for the little lady's purse."

"Better yet," the clean cut guy said as he shot a leering glance at Taryn. "How 'bout we just get you out of the way and we'll take care of the pretty little lady ourselves?"

"I think you guys might have picked the wrong guy to play with."

"Really? And what are you going to do... take us both on?"

Matt rolled his shoulders, shook out his arms and took a solid step toward the pair.

"Matt, don't," Taryn said. "It's not worth getting hurt over. They can have my purse."

Matt simply stared the two young men down. The scruffy guy gaped with disbelief and uncertainty as he backed away while his partner stood his ground a moment longer before also backing away. "You better think twice before you come walking through here again, pretty boy."

Chapter 17

Errol sat sullen in Suzanne's car as she drove them to her apartment to discuss the future of La Benicoise. He knew she had the capacity to put everything back in order, to assuage the disappointed customers booked for the upcoming weeks and to calm his worries. Despite all her capabilities, however, he simply wanted to be with Taryn. He'd tried to call her, but she never picked up.

She'd not waited for him and he wondered why. Of course she had her own restaurant to deal with, but somehow he sensed that wasn't the true reason. He'd seen her speaking to Matt, but more worrisome was what he'd seen in the handsome young fire fighter's eyes. He'd seen the same look on the young chef Henri's face.

"I know this is all a shock, Errol," Suzanne was saying, "but, believe me, this isn't going to stop us. We'll be at the top of the list in no time."

"I have complete faith in you."

She pulled into the parking lot of her building and Errol followed her to her apartment.

"A drink?" she offered.

"Cognac would be nice."

"Be right back."

Errol stood and looked through the window that overlooked the Hudson River. It'd been an eternally long and demanding day. And it wasn't over. Suzanne insisted they look at every reservation to determine how to best deal with some of the more distinguished and demanding patrons.

It'd been a long time since he'd last seen financial woes, and he now feared what lay ahead. It didn't take much to lose a patron. It didn't take long for them to forget and find another restaurant to satisfy their palate.

He'd dug in deep to get the restaurant started. He'd found the perfect piece of real estate, the perfect location and it had cost him plenty. His staff, all highly efficient, had been drilled to suit his demanding pace and he'd prided himself on the finely tuned machine his kitchen was, but would they wait around while he got the restaurant going again?

As his fingers played over the contour of his phone in his pocket, he thought of Taryn. More than anything, he needed to talk to her. He wanted to hear her words of comfort, of reassurance. He wanted to share with her the pain of watching his kitchen go up in flames.

He wanted her... in every way possible.

Five minutes later, Suzanne returned with his brandy. Surprised to see she'd not changed into something frilly and titillating, he took the drink and sat in the lone armchair.

"You looked like you were miles away."

"La Benicoise is my baby. It kills me to see it destroyed."

"It's not destroyed. This is just a little bump in the road, Errol. We'll be up and running faster than you think." She sat on the sofa and leaned forward, her elbows on her knees as she scrutinized him. "What's really on your mind?"

He shrugged. "My original plan was to stay in Paris, to teach." A vision of Taryn came rapidly to his mind as he remembered the first day he met her. "If I hadn't been here..."

"Things would not have been worse. I would've handled things exactly as I did. Admit it; you enjoy being in New York more than Paris. She reached out to put her hand on his knee.

Dropping a sour gaze to her hand, he held back on a grimace and sipped his cognac.

"The institute must be eager to have you back."

He nodded. "They were very understanding when I told them I needed to come here."

Suzanne squeezed his knee and looked pointedly at him. "I'm thrilled you changed your plans and decided to come to New York, but you know as well as I do that you didn't have to come. We didn't need you. Things have been running smoothly for a while and contacting you via emails and the occasional phone call was more than enough."

"You know I'm a hands-on kind of guy."

She let out a sexy chuckle, though her eyes remained hard and inquisitive.

"Why did you really come to New York, Errol?"

"I just told you."

"I know you. You're lying." She sat back and crossed her arms in front of her, pulling on her torn shirt to expose more of her breasts in the process. "You came here because of that silly little cook you're so enchanted with."

Errol glared at her. In no mood to argue, he said, "So what if I did?"

"You must be losing your golden touch. Seems it wasn't too long ago girls all over the world were chasing after you. Now, here you are ready to cross the Atlantic just to be with this one girl."

Swirling the cognac in his glass, he looked intently at the amber liquid. "Maybe it's time," he said softly. "I think I just might be ready to settle down."

A loud guffaw exploded in the room as Suzanne threw her head back and slapped her knee. "You'll never settle down, Errol, especially not with a pixie like her. Be realistic. You get bored with an ordinary woman after only a few months. Do this girl a favor and cut off communications with her now. Leading her on and letting her believe she could actually have a future with you is unfair to the poor thing."

"And since when do you care?"

Her lips took on a sultry grin as her eyes narrowed. "I've always cared, Errol. I know the type of man you are. I know the kind of loving you need. I know how to keep you happy… in every room of the house. Don't you remember how it was, Errol? Don't you remember how great we worked together when you first started plans for La Benicoise? Don't you remember how we'd cap those hard days of work with nights filled with such passion, so much passion you thought you'd explode?"

"I have a wildly colored past. I know that."

Outraged, she got to her feet and tore the remaining tatters of her shirt off. "Are you calling this a colored past?"

Bored, he looked up at her. "Suzanne, I think I've reached a new chapter in my life."

"Yeah, right. That little gnat is an insanely jealous little fiend who won't ever let you out of her sight if you give her that power. Is that what you really want? To be tied down to a woman who'll control you, tell you what you can and can't do?" She let out a sardonic chuckle. "You wouldn't last three days."

Biting his lower lip in concentration, he looked past Suzanne. Yes, Taryn had a few insecurities, but he had to admit, they were well founded where he was concerned. He could certainly understand her lack of faith in him, but he was ready to prove her wrong.

If Taryn was insecure about the women he met on his travels, he'd gladly take her with him everywhere he went. They could travel the world together, and they would share a bed every night.

A slow, pleased grin moved over his lips at the thought.

Suzanne fell to her knees in front of him, a glimmer of desperation in her eyes. "When I first met you, I thought you were arrogant, pretentious and conceited, but I quickly discovered the real man beneath that hardened shell." She trailed one hand over his lap, found the tear that exposed his thigh and slipped her hand inside. "I'd never made love quite the way I did as that first night with you. You brought out the animal in me. You made me feel…"

Gripping her fingers in a tight hold, he stopped her. "We had fun, Suzanne, but now it's over."

"No." She pressed her breasts to his legs.

"Don't."

"You know you can't resist it," she whispered. "The only reason you're so hung up on this girl right now is because she won't have you. Think about it. You have thousands of girls eager to please you and all you want is the one girl who ran away from you. The moment you win her over, the minute you succeed in getting her into your bed again, the thrill will be gone and you'll be on the prowl for the next conquest."

"If that's true, don't you think you've taken the wrong strategy… throwing yourself on your knees before me?"

She swallowed the indignant ball of resentment as her eyes narrowed in scorn. Rolling her tongue around in her mouth, she stood and jutted her chin out. "Believe it or not, Errol, I see us together. I see a future for us, and it's not just sex. We're the perfect professional team. You've even said how many times I've read your mind in the kitchen, knowing ahead of time what you want and need. With the time you'll lose to repair the damages, you can't afford to start looking for a new chef." She looked pointedly at him. "You know you need me in your restaurant."

"Is that a threat?"

"I love you, Errol. While you were in Paris I'd allowed that simmering love to dissipate and I concentrated all my efforts into the running of La Benicoise, but now that you're here… How can I make you see…?"

"You can't, Suzanne." He stood and set his cognac on the end table. "I better go."

"Errol," she called as he walked away. "I swear, if you walk out that door, you'll regret it for the rest of your days. La Benicoise will suffer... your career will suffer. Errol... that amateur chef... that juvenile lover won't satisfy you."

He hailed a cab and gave the driver the address to La Benicoise where he'd left his car. Sitting in the back seat he considered going to Taryn's. Would she be home? Would she be alone?

He wasn't really sure if he wanted to find out. It had gnawed at him since she'd left; the possibility that she'd left with Matt. The handsome young fire fighter had been talking to her when Errol had last seen her. Why? Why would she leave with Matt when he's specifically told her he'd wanted to see her?

Matt was more her age. She'd known him for years, and no doubt he had a less colorful history. Was that really what Taryn wanted? Matt was a good guy, but when it came to Taryn, Errol wanted her all to himself.

He pulled out his phone and sent her a pleading text. By the time his cab had pulled up beside his car, she'd still not answered. He paid his fare and got out. As he debated what to do next, he paced in front of his boarded up restaurant for the next ten minutes.

The thought of losing her killed him. Just the past weeks without her had been torture, and he couldn't bear the thought of living the rest of his life without her. He'd never felt such tenderness, passion, possessiveness, and lust for a woman before.

With a hasty decision made, he got in his car and headed to Taryn's apartment. His heart ached at the thought of what he might find and he wasn't really sure how he'd react if he were to find her alone with Matt.

He parked and noticed that her car wasn't there. Perhaps Matt had brought her home. Maybe he'd gotten her drunk and was now licking her, fucking her, taking what was his.

Don't, he told himself. Don't even go there.

At the door, he listened for a long moment. His heart dropped to the floor as he detected soft and sensual male murmurings and the unmistakable sound of a female giggle.

The lost little boy in him was prepared to declare defeat. He closed his eyes and leaned his forehead against the door frame. He'd lost her. He'd been stupid and selfish, and now she was wrapped up in another man's arms.

"I won't give up that easily," he muttered as he took a deep breath and banged on the door. His heart raced and his breaths came out in short spasms. He tried to swallow, but his mouth was painfully dry.

The murmurs ceased and the giggles subsided, and were followed by a torturous moment of silence. The latch clicked open, the doorknob turned and the door opened.

"Hey, Errol," Bobby said with a lusty grin still plastered to his face. The room behind him was dark save for a few lit candles.

"Bobby," Errol sighed with relief and disbelief. "Bobby, man am I happy to see you." Behind Bobby, he could see a pretty young girl sitting on the sofa, one of the girls who'd been at the seminar, and she eagerly awaited Bobby's return. "I'm so sorry to barge in like this, but... where's Taryn?"

Startled, Bobby looked at him and frowned, and put a silencing finger up to his lips. "My mom's in the next room. I don't want to wake her," he whispered. "What do you mean, where is Taryn? I thought she was with you."

"She stopped by the restaurant earlier, but she left before I could finish up."

"I don't get it. She called me earlier asking if I could cover for her. I assumed it was because she wanted to spend some time with you, what with the fire and all."

Errol felt the ugly grimace work its way over his lips. He'd rarely been given to bouts of jealousy in his life, but now, as he realized she really was with Matt, he was filled with emotions that threatened to tear him apart. "She must've left with her fireman friend."

"Matt?"

"Look, I've left her a few texts and I've left messages. She knew I was distraught over the fire. I'm sure she would have called back if she could have." He knew it was wishful thinking on his part, but he couldn't believe she could so callously ignore his pain right now.

Bobby rushed to the end table, grabbed his phone and dialed. "Taryn, Taryn are you there? Pick up. Taryn, it's Bobby. I need to talk to you, now." With the phone still up to his ear, he looked at Errol with fear in his eyes. "Taryn," he whispered. "Please call me the minute you can."

"Where could they have gone?" Errol said.

Bobby shrugged. "I know Matt mentioned taking her out before, but..." Clasping his hands, he said, "Oh, I know. The other day he mentioned taking her to this pizzeria... Joe's I think. They used to hang out there when they were teens and he thought it'd be a great place to reminisce."

"If he did take her there, he's nuts. That neighborhood turned sour a few years back. It's not a place to go wandering at night."

Bobby turned to the quiet and disappointed girl on the couch. "I'm sorry. I really have to go." He gazed down as her state of semi-dress. "Let yourself out when you're ready."

She nodded as Bobby grabbed his jacket and ushered Errol out.

Errol drove at breakneck speed. He was eager to find Taryn, but also hoped to attract the attention of the police. If something had happened, they'd need all the help they could get.

They arrived at Joe's and parked the car.

"There," Bobby said as he pointed across the street. "That's Matt's car."

Could they still be at the pizzeria? Errol wondered. Had it been one of those long and luscious nights of talking about old times, getting reacquainted and connecting all over again?

He rushed to the door of Joe's. "Have you guys seen a really pretty young woman come in here with a tall young man?"

"A young couple came in to have a pizza," the waiter said. "They must have left, what, five or ten minutes ago."

"Thanks." Standing out on the sidewalk, he looked at Bobby with a helpless sense of desperation. "Matt's car is there, but they're not. They couldn't possibly have gone for a walk, not here. It'd be suicide."

In the moment he spoke, he heard a disturbing cry from the alley across the street. With Bobby at his heels, he ran to the source of the cry and found a scene even more disturbing that seeing Taryn in another man's arms.

Lying on her back, she screamed as the scumbag sitting atop her grabbed her neck with his filthy fist while he tore her shirt open with grubby and eager fingers. Beyond them, Matt struggled with another young and angry man.

Without taking a second to consider his options, he jumped the guy on Taryn while Bobby tackled Matt's attacker.

"Hey, what the...?" Taryn's assailant cried out as he was jerked off her thrashing body. He tried to throw a punch back at Errol, but the blood flow to his arms didn't seem quite adequate. Lust and anger burned in his eyes a moment before he finally managed to focus on Errol's face.

Chapter 18

Breathless as she ran a soothing hand over her aching neck, Taryn sat up the moment the weight of her attacker was taken off her.

The attack had happened so fast. Matt had turned to open the car door for her and she'd hurried inside, eager to get away from the unwelcoming neighborhood, but before Matt could close the door, one of the guys came back and jumped on Matt while his friend jerked Taryn out of the car and dragged her to the nearby alley.

Kicking and screaming she'd tried to fend him off, but he'd quickly thrown her to the ground and given her a resounding smack on the cheek. Stunned, she'd remained silent for one frozen moment, painfully aware of the struggle Matt was having with the dirty fighter he was confronted with.

But when her assailant tore her shirt open and exposed her, she'd let out a panicked cry.

Now as she watched Errol, barely recognizing him with the murderous fury in his eyes, she feared for him.

While the two young men had initially been intimidating in a juvenile sort of way, they had quickly proven to be violent in their attack.

Errol, however, quickly showed her just how strong and determined he was by pulling a punch that wiped the focus right out of the greasy guy's gaze. The guy fell back and wiped the blood from under his nose with the back of his hand.

For a moment, she thought the fight would end there, but he got back on his feet and pulled a knife out as he ran to Errol. Taryn let out a frantic yelp, but just as Errol deftly sidestepped his attacker and twisted his arm painfully behind his back, another cry caught her attention.

Bobby fought the taller of the two punks with surprising ease and strength while Matt lay sprawled on the ground, blood seeping from a wound on his head. She'd never seen Bobby so angry and couldn't help but wonder where all the rage came from. Regardless of the punches and kicks he gave the guy, however, the persistent attacker continued to come back for more.

Taryn didn't know where to turn; her lover, brother and friend were all in danger and there seemed no end to the attacker's ferocity.

Sirens blared in the distance and Taryn breathed her first sigh of relief since stepping out of Joe's. But before the police arrived three cars screeched to a stop and out popped half a dozen photographers.

"Errol, over here," one shouted as he snapped a shot of Errol pushing his punk up to the wall.

"Let him have it, Errol," another one said.

All eager to get a shot of the famed chef in all his raging glory, they pressed closer and closer.

"This is no place for paparazzi, guys," Errol growled. "Why not give us a hand instead."

"Looks like you got everything under control, chef."

While Errol did have his assailant under control, Bobby still fought, each punch and kick echoing in the alley. The groans and moans of fighting fell silent, however, when the punk stabbed Bobby in the abdomen.

"The bitch wasn't worth it anyway," he muttered as he ran out of the alley leaving his friend to deal with the cops on his own.

Taryn let out a horrified scream as she scrabbled to get to her feet to help her brother.

The paparazzi clicked away, unfazed by the violence and blood... all except one who dared put his camera down and come to Bobby's aid.

"Get away from him," Taryn cried as she took Bobby's hand in hers.

"I've got my first responders certification," he said. "Let me help him until the ambulance gets here."

Frantic, she nodded as she saw the blood flow out of her brother. "Please, do whatever you can."

The photographers continued to take shot after shot; Errol, his clothes tattered and torn, and his face contorted in rage; Taryn, her shirt torn open and exposing far too much of her breasts as she cried over her bloodied brother. The scene was impossible to fathom, obscene in its ridicule. How could they just stand there and take pictures?

When the police arrived, they managed to finally get the last of the paparazzi cleared away. As the medics rolled Matt and Bobby into the ambulance, Errol came up behind Taryn and put his hand on her shoulder.

Chapter 19

Taryn sat staring straight ahead as Errol drove through the streets of New York. It had been a day she'd always remember, though she fervently wished she could forget it all. Though Matt had been released after only an hour, Bobby had been admitted to the hospital.

In a turmoil filled with confusion, pain and anger, Taryn had silently watched Matt walk out of the hospital, his understanding of the situation plain on his face.

Guilt boiled in her belly, turning it upside down as she berated herself for bringing him into her sordid and pathetic life. She'd been angry and hurt and should have gone home alone instead of using Matt to assuage her broken heart.

"We're home," Errol softly said as he parked the car.

He guided her into his apartment, and after he closed the door, she turned to look at him, letting out a sardonic laugh.

"Look at us," she said.

Errol looked down at the clothes on his back, clothes that now hung like rags over his shoulders. Between the fire and the fight, little remained of what had been a perfect suit that very morning.

He gazed at Taryn with an amused smirk. Though she hadn't had a good look at herself, she could just imagine how messed up she looked. Her hair felt dirty and stringy as it fell around her face and her hands, despite having washed them, were still sticky and grimy.

At the hospital she'd temporarily managed to keep her shirt decent and pinned up with a paperclip, but she'd lost it and was once again daringly exposed.

"Yes," he said with an unsure grin. "Look at us."

They stared at each other for a long silent moment.

"We've been through a lot together," he said.

Taryn looked around the posh apartment, making them look all the more ridiculous in their dirty and torn clothes. She realized after a thorough look around that she'd expected to see signs of Suzanne. "I think I should go home, Errol. I don't belong here."

"More than ever, you belong here."

"I'm not so sure."

"Look, your mother is home and sleeping. Do you really think you'd be doing her a favor by arriving in the state you're in? And having to explain, in the middle of the night, what happened to Bobby?"

"You always have the winning argument, don't you?"

With an uncharacteristically shy smile, he reached for her hand and led her to the bathroom. "If nothing else, let's get you cleaned up and presentable."

He helped her out of her rags, tore off what remained of his own clothing and opened the door to the large shower stall.

Taryn hesitated a moment before stepping into the shower. She knew very well where it could lead.

"I'm not going to bite," he said as he nudged her in.

With a turn of a few knobs, he had water gushing out of a dozen shower heads, two on top and three sets of three all around the shower stall. The spray was refreshing and strangely energizing.

Errol squirted a lightly scented body gel onto a soft, thick washcloth and slowly washed the grime of the day off Taryn.

"Why did you leave?" he said softly as he washed her back.

She tilted her head down, letting the water spill over her head. "I was tired of seeing how Suzanne hung all over you."

"I needed you."

Her heart swelled and tears quickly blurred her vision. He kissed the tender skin of the shoulder he'd just washed.

"I need you." He wrapped his arm around her waist and pressed his chest to her back.

It would be so easy to give way to her emotions, to melt into him and open her heart, but she knew where he was going. With a cynical gleam in her eye, she looked over her shoulder at him while reaching back to grab his erection.

"I know," she said, her voice strangely flat and cold.

He gently removed her hand and turned her to face him. "That's not what I need. I want it. I want it all the time. I want you, your hands, your mouth." He leaned in to passionately kiss her. "Your tongue. I want it all... all the time. But... I need you, Taryn. Until this morning when that fire broke out, I hadn't really realized just how desperately I needed you. You were the first one I wanted to talk to, to share my heartache with."

Inhaling deeply, she looked up at him. Water trickled through his hair, over his face and fell in delectable drops along his torso. She wanted to believe him, to believe his feelings for her ran deeper than just sexual.

"I'm sorry. I really wished I would have stayed with you." She shrugged. "I guess I kind of panicked. Suzanne is very…"

"Suzanne is the last thing I want to think or talk about." He set his hand on the wall of the shower and leaned into her. His kiss was slow and hot, drawing her out, one tantalizing lick at a time. He didn't reach for a breast, or press his chest to hers, but simply kissed her with such tenderness and affection.

Aroused to the point of feeling weak on her feet, Taryn leaned into him. With a slight sense of deviance and a large dose of hunger, she pressed her breasts to his chest as she wrapped her arms around him. Her hands trailed down to grab his buttocks and press his hips to hers.

Staying close, Errol looked into her eyes. "You excite me today just as much as you did that first day. I still thrill at the sight of seeing your exquisite body. I still delight in the touch of your skin. If anything, I find myself wanting you more and more."

To emphasize his words, his hard erection slid between her legs and glided along her feminine folds. After a few slow and arousing strokes, he wrapped his arms around her and slid down until his face was in her crotch. "I want you more and more," he whispered as he kissed the tender skin.

His tongue and lips worked together to bring her to excruciating heights of arousal, but he artfully managed to keep her just one step away from reaching a full orgasm. The sensations blotted out everything else around her, leaving her body feeling light, almost numb.

"You're going to kill me," she whispered as she dug her fingers through his hair and pressed his face closer to her.

Chapter 20

Taryn lay on her side and stared at the wall as Errol slept, his body pressed up against her back. The sun threw its first early morning shadows on the ceiling. Their night of passion, of endless lovemaking had reminded her just how much she loved him... and all that passion had let the words slip off her tongue. She could still see the expression on his face when she'd told him she loved him; confusion, uncertainty, and suspicion.

How stupid can you be? she'd told herself. My God, how many times had he heard women telling him they loved him? Hundreds? Thousands? And here she was, just another dimwit who didn't realize the basis of their relationship. Sex.

Errol's phone rang, and Taryn closed her eyes, feigning sleep.

"Oui. Pourquoi? Non, ah merde."

Though she had no idea what he was talking about, she could tell he was unhappy with this unexpected call from France.

"Quand?" he said. Getting out of bed, he went to his dresser and picked up the small calendar. *"Pas vrai."*

Cracking her eyes open, she saw his agitation, and wondered who he was speaking to.

"Merde, de merde," he muttered as he hung up and tossed the phone to the floor.

Taryn sat up and looked at him. "I didn't want to eavesdrop, but I couldn't help but hear how upset you are."

"My idiot of a manager. He knows how busy I've been here, but he decides to contact me at the last minute to tell me I have to be in Paris… tomorrow."

Her heart sank at the thought of him leaving.

"With the restaurant down for a few weeks, things are going to get rough. I have a contract with those people in Paris. If I don't show up they'll sue the tattered pants right off me. I can't afford to do anything stupid right now."

"You have no choice, then. You have to go, Errol. If you want, I can keep an eye on things here… make sure everything is moving along at La Benicoise."

"Really? You'd do that for me? I could be gone for a few weeks, maybe a month."

A month? She didn't know how she could bare having him out of her life for an entire month. It seemed so eternally long. "Of course," she said with a bright smile. "As a restaurateur, I know how it is to see your baby down and out."

He knelt in front of her and took her hands in his. "You have no idea how much I appreciate your offer."

She smiled, hiding her heartache. She didn't want her insecurities to get the best of her, but she felt the stirrings of jealousy rise again.

"But the truth is I have another favor to ask you."

"Sure, I'll do whatever I can to help."

"Come with me."

"Okay," she got up and prepared to follow him.

"No," he said with an amused chuckle. "Not here. Paris."

"What?" she murmured in disbelief. "Paris?"

"Come to Paris with me. In a way, the timing couldn't be more perfect. My whole team will be out of work for the next weeks as the Benicoise gets back on its feet. They can keep busy at Sam's. It'll give your mom and Bobby time to recover, and you can come be a real help to me."

"Errol, I don't know…"

"You know how my guys loved working at Sam's. A few of them already know the drill. They won't let you down."

"It's not that. Errol, Bobby's just been stabbed and my mom still needs help at home. I can't just go off to Paris to… to do what?"

"Be with me," he said as he squeezed her hands. "Just be with me, Taryn."

"It doesn't make sense, Errol. What am I going to do in Paris while you're off taping your show? Wait around your apartment just so we can fuck at night when you arrive?"

He frowned. "I know our relationship has largely been sex driven, and yes…" He cocked his brow. "I will want to fuck you every night when I get home, but I will also want to wake up beside you every morning. I'll want to go take long walks with you in the park. I'll want to sit in the tub and talk to you about my day, and hear about yours. And I want everything else in between. You know, in all my travels around the world, no matter how elegant the hotel suite, no matter how enchanting the villa, I've never felt at home." He brought her hand to his cheek then kissed her palm. "You make me feel at home, Taryn. No matter where I am, if I'm with you, I feel like I'm home."

Strong emotions choked her as she looked into his eyes and tried to blink away the tears that filled her own.

Unexpectedly, he rose and walked to his dresser where he opened a drawer, retrieved something and returned to kneel before her.

"The first time I saw that picture of you, the one you sent in to the institute with your application form, I knew... I knew I wanted to know you. And when I first saw you in the flesh..." He bit his lip and shook his head as his gaze traveled leisurely over her naked body. "I'll admit I've known a lot of women in my life, Taryn, but I'd never felt the way I did that very first time with you, and that feeling has grown these past months. You're like a piece of the puzzle that's always been missing. You make me feel whole and you have a way of bringing light into a life that's always been so dark. When I saw you on your back last night, with that idiot's hand on your neck... I swear, Taryn, I could have killed him."

He pulled up the small box he'd kept behind his back.

Taryn's eyes widen before glistening with unshed tears.

Epilogue

After the hectic lunch hour rush at Sam's, Taryn washed her hands and gazed once again at the antique diamond ring on her hand. It had belonged to Errol's grandmother... his nana, and Taryn cherished it all the more for the history and love the ring represented. She still couldn't believe Errol's proposal. It'd been a surprise and a shock. It'd been everything she'd wanted.

In the end, however, going off to Paris was something she knew she couldn't do. Her mother needed her, and though Bobby was already going strong and flirting with every nurse who dared entered his room, he wouldn't be back at work for another week.

"That's quite a rock you've got there," Arnie said as he came up to the sink to wash his hands. "You've been looking at it every chance you get."

"Yeah," she said as she held up her hand to get a better look. "I guess I am a little star struck. I've never seen anything more beautiful." While she let Arnie think she was referring to the fabulous ring, in her mind's eye she could clearly see Errol's face, his eyes filled with hope and anticipation in the seconds that had preceded her acceptance of his proposal.

Since his departure three days earlier, Errol had sent countless texts and had called her every night.

"He's a real lucky guy," Arnie said. "I hope you two will be happy."

"Thanks, Arnie. That's really sweet."

As he walked away, she turned and looked at the team of workers around her. A few of Errol's employees had come to lend a hand and they blended perfectly with her own team. For all the tragedy that had seemed to dog her recently, she felt proud, strong and happy.

Her phone buzzed, indicating another text message.

Hey, honey... I was working on a particular recipe today and thought specifically of you. I had to use a lemon reamer and it brought back great memories.

Taryn blushed as she remembered how Errol had used a lemon reamer on her. It had been an exciting night.

Production on the show is running smoothly. A lot of people have been commenting on my behavior. They all noticed how uncharacteristically cheery I am. Seems I'm radiating joy.

I hope you have no doubt that it's all because of you. I'm happy and it shows. I'm relaxed, despite the hectic schedule. I'm in love and I can't hide it.

I can't wait to see you soon. Love, Errol.

Consume Me (Volume 3, Master Chefs Series)

September 2013

A Sneak Peak at:

The Innocent

The Protege #2

Kailin Gow

Prologue

Serena ran through the school as fast as her four inch heels and pencil skirt permitted. It was impossible to be discreet as her heels clicked loudly on the tiled floor of the deserted hall and she felt certain every student in every class could hear her pass by. Everyone was already in their classes where they belonged; everyone except Serena who was thirty minutes late for her very first class.

She pulled open the door to the grand lecture hall and quietly found a seat at the back of the room. Breathless and eager to catch up on what she'd missed, she pulled out her laptop and took notes.

Her quick and quiet entrance, however, didn't go unnoticed by the devastatingly handsome man speaking to the class. He stopped speaking for the slightest second, a pause barely perceptible, but Serena noticed. She also noticed the longing gaze he briefly directed at her.

"Inspiration comes in many forms," he said. "Tragedy and heartache have inspired countless melancholy melodies, whereas joy and romance have brought about beautiful music; music that lifts the spirit; music that brings on the desire to love."

Serena typed out every word, all while keeping her eyes steadily on him. When his gaze swept across the room and stopped to connect with hers for the briefest moment, she didn't see the masterful composer who spoke so eloquently about his passion for music, but a man who loved and needed love. Even with a room full of students between them, she felt his love.

"Some dare say," he went on, "if you've not lived, if you've not lost, you cannot compose great music. True, a life rich with experience, pain and pleasure, gain and loss, love and hate, can beget profound melodies that evoke strong emotions even from the coldest and disinterested listener. However, this doesn't preclude you, young and virginal, green and pure, to compose beautiful music. Everyone has a past, be it filled with sorrow or joy, pride or regret. Don't be afraid to dig deep, to go behind doors you may have closed, to re-open old wounds you'd rather forget. Pour them out onto that blank sheet of paper staring back at you."

He turned his back on the room and walked to the piano set behind him. Sitting down, he looked at the room of eager students. "If you would humor me, please close your eyes, listen, and allow your emotions to take over."

With one finger, he tapped on a solitary low note for two measures before adding a slow and dramatic melody.

Serena closed her eyes and listened to every note. She could almost hear his voice calling out to her as his fingers played along the lower register of the piano. She could almost hear his heart break.

The melody ached, broke and fell apart with devastating heartache. As the song went on, brooding and dark, she heard a few sniffles, a few whimpers and finally a soft sob.

When Sebastian rested his fingers over the stilled keys of the piano, the room was silent save for the quiet sobs. Serena opened her eyes and caught Sebastian's poignant gaze, a gaze filled with the very emotions his composition evoked. His blue eyes held her, mesmerized as the emotions filled her.

"Now," Sebastian said with a clap of his hands. He cleared his throat and stood before the class. "Looking at you, I can see there's plenty of emotion in the room. What did you feel?"

"Sad," many students said at once.

"Yes," Sebastian said. "I guess there is something rather sad about it. Anything else?"

"The rhythm was almost plaintive, as if the piano was crying."

"Some of the combinations of low base notes with the high, sharp ones added something mysterious and enigmatic to the melody."

"I felt sad, almost morose throughout the song, but in the end, it seemed to hold a faint note of hope."

Sebastian cocked his brow. "Interesting. So we have a sad mystery with a grain of hope."

"Where did you get the inspiration for such a composition?" a young woman in the front row said.

Wringing his hands together, Sebastian shot a wicked grin around the large room. He inhaled deeply as he hesitated. "All I'll say is, when you find love, true love, hold onto it, because once you let go, it can easily become your greatest regret in life."

"Are you in love with someone you can't have?" another girl asked.

He grinned and clucked his tongue. "I'm happy to see my music touched you all as intended. Think about what you can bring to your own compositions and I'll see you all tomorrow."

Having dismissed the question and the class, Sebastian picked up his notes and jacket as students cleared the room. With the room almost empty, he walked to the back of the class to Serena.

"You came in late."

"There was more traffic than I anticipated." She slipped her laptop into her bag and pulled the strap over her shoulder. "I'll make sure I leave home earlier tomorrow."

"You look lovely today – surprisingly prim and proper. I'll admit you're just as alluring buttoned up to the collar as you are in the nude. There's something naughty behind that crisp blue shirt that makes me want to tear it off."

"That wasn't my intention. I wanted to show you I'm serious about my music."

He grinned. "Speaking of which... I need to see you in my office. I want to discuss my expectations. As your advisor, I won't tolerate tardiness, or laziness."

"Yes, Sir." Serena followed him out of the lecture hall.

His strides were long and forceful as he walked out of the building and into the neighboring one where his office was housed. On entering the building, she remembered her first encounter with him. How quickly they'd grown close. How quickly she'd developed such intense affection for him.

Now, as he pushed the door open to let her into his office, she knew she wouldn't have the strength to resist him should he touch her.

"You know how I feel about tardiness." His voice was hard with scorn as he closed the door behind them.

Book 2 of The Protégé, The Innocent is set to release August 26, 2013

Another Steamy Adult Novel from Kailin Gow

Bestselling Novel…now available!

The Protégé

She was the young promising composer in search of a master to teach her and advise her. Serena Singleton was the beautiful up and coming talent brought to the attention of the eccentric, famous, and wildly wealthy Sebastian Sorenson, one of the foremost and most talented composers in Hollywood and in the Academics field. A chance encounter brings them into an arrangement that turns out beyond their expectations and desire, testing their boundaries. Who is the student, the protege, and who is the teacher? Nothing is as it seems in this romantic exotic thriller.

A New Steamy Series from Kailin Gow

For 18+ due to strong sexual situations and mature subject matter

The Blue Room Trilogy

The Blue Room, an erotic nightclub where the rich and famous go to experience their wildest fantasies, is also the new responsibility of Terrence Blue, the bad boy bastard son of billionaire eccentric Clarence Blue. Terrence, only in his mid-twenties, still has wild oats to sow, drunken parties to attend, and women who bed. Running the exclusive luxury club where discretion is the top priority, then come pleasure, was not what Terrence had planned. He was a client himself, and wanted to stay one, having found his fame and fortune on screen, as one of the biggest stars in the adult films; but finding out that he was son to Clarence Blue, changed all that.

A lot goes on behind the doors of The Blue Room…pleasure, fantasy, betrayal, guilt, and decadence. Everything Terrence is used to, but he never expected that he would find love, too, especially from the least expected...

Get a Free Full-length Book when you subscribe to Kailin's newsletter!

https://dl.bookfunnel.com/5rmis5rrj1